I0718722

Ocean's Gift

DEMELZA CARLTON

DEDICATION

This book is dedicated to Arielle for reminding me that mermaids are silly.

SIRENA

The ocean gave him to me.

I was angry, as any girl of sixteen would be. I'd been ordered by my elders to go and find a strong man, one I could join with to produce a healthy child. My hopes, my dreams and my plans were of no consequence. My destiny was to entice a man to choose me as his plaything – to be a piece of flesh to bait a shark. Or to be a baby seal, tempting a killer whale? The example did not matter. The end would be the same – the end of my control over what had been my life.

I swam in the storm, revelling in the power of the waves, which pushed a little wooden sailing boat through the maelstrom on the surface over my head. Two men struggled to control the small craft with two wooden oars, the vessel's only means of propulsion once the sail was torn away in the wind. One man dived from the boat, slicing into the water like a knife surrounded by bubbles. There was a line of twisted fibre in his hand as he swam with difficulty for shore.

The little boat rocked in reaction to the diver's spring. The wind caught the remnants of the sail, a big wave washed over the side and the vessel tipped under the surface, sinking slowly. I dodged through the debris as it drifted in the current away from the little boat.

The surface above me churned where the second man had been thrown into the water. He thrashed around and it was clear he could not swim. The waves pushed us together and he clung to me, his arms warm as he wrapped them around me. I gave him my breath and took him to the surface. As we drifted between the waves, still he would not let me go.

He called me his Lady of the Sea, his angel. I gave him my breath again, before I dove under the waves with him.

We surfaced near a small island of sand, washed by the waves. Here he would be safe.

He shivered, in wet clothes on wet sand. He called me Santa Maria, his Star of the Sea who had answered his prayer.

If I was to save him, I had to keep him warm. Yet I had no human accoutrements, nothing warm or dry with which to assist him. Only me.

I concentrated on my form, letting my tail part, my skin pale and my gills fade. To save this man, I needed to be human.

Or as close as I could be.

He kissed and clung to the naked human girl by his side, who could think of only one way to warm him. He kissed my lips and my blood responded with a wave of heat, akin in power to the waves of the storm on my body.

We warmed one another, as the storm and the waves raged around us. He clung to me even when exhaustion claimed us.

When I awoke, the storm had dissipated. I could return this man to his people and he would live.

Whilst he still slept, I carried him through the water to the island where his kind lived. Yet in the deep water there were sharks, attracted by the man's blood.

Mine.

Leaving him floating on the surface, I charged the sharks, shouting my claim to drive them off. It came to blows to drive the last one away, before I could return for my human.

Yet he was not on the surface when I returned. The water in his clothing had dragged him down, into the deep where he could not breathe. I gave him my breath, over and over, in a poor, cold imitation of his ardent kisses, yet I could breathe no life into his body.

The ocean gave me this man, his life to save, then stole his breath even as I tried to save him. The man who called me an angel, Maria, as he loved me for a storm.

I cursed the islands, for they were cursed already. I would not go ashore on these wretched rocks, to conceive a child to take back to my sisters in the deep. No child conceived in such bitterness would survive inside me to be birthed at the Nursery Grounds. So I resolved to tell my elders, when I returned to them.

I cannot carry a child for you. Even the ocean is against it.

In a sea of rebelliousness, the girl he called Maria was lost, as I turned tail and dove deep.

JOE

I like setting up remote mining camps. Inland Western Australia is one of the few places in the world where you can drive out of civilisation in the morning and know you're in the middle of nowhere when you stop at the end of the day.

I'd arrive at a cleared site, where the carpenters were just putting together the construction camp buildings we called dongas, and when I left it was almost ready for the mining crew to live in. We were creating civilisation where there had been nothing, just plants, animals and red dust. And when the mining crew left, we'd pull the camps apart like

Lego and pack them up to be shifted somewhere else on the back of a truck. The plants and animals would move back in around and under the buildings while we were there and they'd reclaim it completely when we left. The red dust was ever-present. You never got rid of it, because it got everywhere and into everything.

The bad part was that the camps weren't inhabitable until we finished. So, while we worked, we lived rough. We were the last people who actually camped there. We slept in swags and cooked outside, in the beam of the spotlights on the top of the car, which was a ute. There was one ute to two men, and I shared mine with Dean the plumber. Dean was full of shit, so it seemed natural that he was a plumber. Still, he was a better cook than me and a good mate, too.

Our supplies were packed into the tray on the back of the ute and the trailer behind it. We had enough for the job and a bit over, but never enough water for much more than drinking and cooking. After a week, we were all dreaming about hot showers.

Like all the other mine construction crews, we had to go back to town eventually and we got to stay in a hotel for the night, before they flew us all home. It was a ritual by now. I checked into the hotel with all the other blokes who were covered in red dust. I got my room and I got to shut the door to everyone else. Then I took a shower.

After endless weeks of basic camps, where sometimes the best wash you got was a swim in the river, the hotel shower was heaven. I used up all the hot water and all the liquid soap, just to get the gritty feeling of red dust off every bit of my skin. Shit, it felt good. Almost better than sex.

Which I haven't had for longer than I've been without a hot shower. I tried not to think about it. Now I was going to have some holidays in civilisation, who knew what would happen?

I slept in silence and darkness. When I opened my eyes, the sun was up.

I got dressed quickly, my legs feeling bare in shorts after so long in site pants that kept out the sun and the snakes. Even a short-sleeved t-shirt felt weird. My feet felt like they'd been freed from prison in my rubber thongs, after weeks of thick socks and work boots.

I crossed the car park from my room to the hotel restaurant for breakfast. I wasn't the only one dressed this casual. Most of the guys were the same, toes wiggling in relief under every table. Anywhere else, this might be strange. In a mining town, it was normal.

"Hey, morning, Joe!" Dean the plumber called from a table by the window. After working on the same crew so long, I should have been sick of him, but I was in such a good mood I'd put up with him one more morning over breakfast.

"Morning," I responded. I went up to the breakfast buffet and grabbed a plate, loading it up with as much as I could. I dumped it on the table, in front of the seat across from Dean, and sat down.

"Coffee, sir?" A waitress came up behind me with an electronic order pad.

My mouth watered. I'm not sure if it was her or the thought of real coffee that did it. *Probably the coffee*, I decided. The waitress looked like she was sixteen and fresh off the farm, dark roots showing through her bleach-blonde hair. *Too young for me – I'm more than ten years older than she is. Besides, she looks like my sister.*

"I want a proper espresso, so thick the spoon almost stands up by itself, and after that, I want a latte," I told her.

"Two coffees, sir?" The little waitress looked confused, which made her slightly cross-eyed.

"Ohhh, yes," I replied. *Definitely the coffee. Her boobs are too small. I like bigger boobs than that.*

I started shovelling breakfast into my mouth, barely tasting it. What I did taste was good, though.

I'd finished my first plate and filled up a second by the time my espresso arrived, in a tiny cup. I savoured every sip until it was gone.

Dean was just as focused on his own breakfast, so it's not like I was being rude. Besides, what else did we have to say, after months of having no one else to talk to?

He laughed at my expression as I enjoyed the espresso. "So, now you've had your coffee, what do you plan to do with your two months off?"

"I'm not sure," I said slowly. I shoved the last half a croissant in my mouth.

"I'm going to go home, get drunk every night in a different pub and see how many hot chicks I can pull, before we're back in the middle of nowhere again." He looked dreamy. "How about you?"

He'll be lucky if he manages to talk even one of them into sleeping with him, I thought. *And I'll be hearing about how hot she was for the whole of the next shift, and how she did everything in every porn movie he's ever watched, which she won't. When he gets sick of that, he'll tell me the plot of every porn film he's ever watched, in his own words. There's nothing worse than a badly told story with no plot and nothing but descriptions of imaginary sex no one could ever have.*

I swallowed the last of my croissant. "Nah, I want to go on a fishing charter, one of those boats that just go out and fish for a week. Then I guess I'll see if I can pick up a bit more work, rewiring people's houses and stuff to get some more money, until we head out to the next hole in the ground to set up camp."

"You work too hard. You have no fun at all,

mate. Still living at home, what are you saving your money for?"

"When I've got enough, I'm going to buy a house outright. Then I'll look at settling down, maybe finding someone to spend the rest of my life with. Maybe even have a family." *Two years and I'll have enough money to buy a house. Then I can finally move out of my parents' place and start living. I'll never have to spend another night listening to other men snoring, or share breakfast with fuckwits like Dean.*

"You need to enjoy life, brother. Have a good time." Dean winked.

"You're not my brother." *Thank God for that.* "And I am going to enjoy my time off. I'm going to spend at least a week fishing, once I work out how to arrange a charter," I reminded him.

"I got a cousin who does some charter fishing out at the Abrolhos. Best fishing of your life, off the coast of Geraldton. I'll give him a call, see if I can set you up," he promised.

Yeah, and pigs will fly.

"Well, you know my number, mate. Give

me a call if your cousin has room for one more on a fishing charter."

I finished off the last bite of bacon, then slurped up a big mouthful of latte. After the espresso, it tasted like a warm coffee milkshake. *I should have ordered two espressos instead.*

"See you at the next site, mate," I told him, getting up. *Only two more years of this and I won't have to say that.* In the meantime, I had a plane to catch back home to Perth.

SIRENA

"We have sisters across the Indian Ocean. We are collecting as much information as we can beneath the surface." It was Elder Darma who'd spoken, but the members of the Elder Council looked to me.

I replied in our language of sounds and gestures that differed so much from human languages. Even translated, the meaning lost its depth in the humans' words. *"This will not be enough. We must discover what the humans know of the subsea disturbances, the changes in flows. They have technology we do not and their information is valuable."*

Elder Cantrella was abrupt as she broke in. *"Elder Sirena, you are our liaison between our people and the humans. What action do you recommend with regard to gathering information from humans?"*

I drew a deep breath of cool water before I responded, for even my recommendations would hold the force of law. "*I would send three parties, small groups who have experience living on land with humans. One to the western coasts, one to the northern and one to the eastern coasts. I recommend we target the countries of South Africa, Singapore and Australia, in each of these regions. Each party may be required to remain for some time on land and give the humans the impression that they are human, too. Throughout, the existence of our people must remain hidden from the humans. Each party must take care to hide the ocean's gift from humans."*

"A difficult task. Whom do you suggest we send?" Elder Darma murmured.

My reply was immediate, for I had considered the matter carefully in the days prior to this meeting. "*For South Africa, I would send Nafula. She has knowledge of the western coasts. For the northern coasts, I would send Indah. I will choose the eastern coasts and Australia for myself, for that is where I suspect the greatest information will be available and that is where I have ties to the human world. Each should choose perhaps one or two to accompany them; I recommend younger sisters who are not yet elders. I shall be accompanied by Maria and Apalala."*

Elder Darma was the facilitator of the Elder Council, though I was its undisputed leader. Custom decreed that she made the final decisions. *"Then it shall be so. You must leave soon, for time is of the essence. I fear great changes are happening in our ocean and the ocean's gift alone may not ensure our survival. We need greater knowledge than we yet have. Without this knowledge, how do we prepare for the worst?"*

The purpose of a leader is both to lead and reassure. I knew my role, for it had been mine for many years now. *"Such knowledge will be obtained and then put to use. We will ensure the survival of our people and of the ocean's gift."*

JOE

As soon as people found out I was back in Perth, I was subcontracting for another electrician I'd apprenticed with, installing air conditioning units, new lights and safety switches. I thought about the fishing charter I wanted to do, but couldn't decide which one. Especially if I could get enough work in that week to get my house sooner. *Fishing can wait, if it means one less shift listening to Dean's fantasies. He always claims they really happened, but if he's telling the truth, he's had more sex than a porn star.*

My phone rang. "Hello, this is Joe," I answered automatically. I pulled a notepad out of the glove box of my ute, clicking a pen in readiness.

"Mate, it's Dean."

Speak of the devil.

"I finally heard from my cousin, the one with the charter boat." He sounded excited.

Please, don't let him want to come with me.

"One of his crew got injured, so he's a man short during the fishing season. He won't be doing charters for a few months, until he gets a new deckhand and finishes fishing up his quota." Dean didn't sound too depressed for me or his cousin.

"Oh, that's too bad. Don't worry about it." I dismissed it. I never thought he or his cousin would come through with anything.

"How'd you like to fish for two months and get paid for it?" Dean burst out.

"What?" *This has got to be a joke. It's Dean, after all.*

"I'm serious. My cousin's a real experienced fisherman and he needs a deckhand for the rest of the season, the next two months. The pay's good and all you have to do is fish." He sounded thrilled at the prospect.

"Why don't you do it? He's your cousin," I

wondered aloud. *There has to be a catch.*

Dean was so excited, he was probably telling the truth without realising. "He won't have me. I was over there for Easter last year and he told me if I got seasick on his boat again he'd throw me over the side for the sharks."

I like his cousin already.

"So I told him about you. You told me you know your way around a boat, and he thinks you'll be perfect!"

I hesitated. He probably sold me as the descendant of Captain Cook, Columbus and Captain Jack Sparrow. "Now look, crewing a boat out to Rottnest and some kayaking on the Swan River isn't like handling a fishing boat offshore..."

"Nah mate, you'll be great. You'll get to go fishing every day, your food and accommodation are provided, what else could you ask for?" Dean sounded like he was trying to sell it to me.

The certainty that you didn't just pull this out of your arse?

"Look, he needs someone as soon as possible. How soon can you get up here?"

Dean's in Geraldton, then.

"I could finish up at the end of the week and fly up on Sunday," I told him reluctantly.

"Cool, I'll get my cousin to sort out your flights and he'll meet you out on the islands. You can see how it goes the first week and if it works out you get paid to go fishing for the rest of your holidays. Seeya." He hung up.

Shit. What've I got myself into? Knowing Dean, this was going to be a disaster. *Oh well, next trip I can always get back at him by putting huge spiders in his swag.* He's terrified of them, but he always forgets to zip his swag up properly. And he screams like a girl when he finds them, too.

What's the worst that can happen? A week on a free fishing charter and possibly getting paid to fish for weeks after it. And if it didn't work out, the next three months of seeing Dean do a high-pitched jig every night when he found spiders in his swag. Hell, there wasn't a downside that I could see.

I started writing down a list of things to pack.

SIRENA

The voyage was long and arduous. After consideration, I'd chosen the very islands I'd cursed as a child as the best starting point to gather information. I had visited them in the interim, but it was my first, stormy swim that came to mind as we approached the continental shelf.

It was a stunning contrast to my first lone swim to land. Much time had passed and I was now an elder, acting under my own command. The two sisters who followed me were my daughters, both adults who had done their duty to our people. The contrast between us was distinctive, too. I twisted to look back.

Over my own blue tail, which blended with the shallow waters at the islands, I could see dark Maria, with her dark blue tail. Apalala was my golden girl, more than ever. The pale yellow tail she had been born with had deepened to gold now. The only brighter tail I had seen was her daughter's, an orange flame that matched her fire-coloured hair. Zerafina had been too young for such a trip, without the assistance of currents to carry us, and our duty too dangerous.

Should the humans discover what we were, we would protect our sisters at all costs. Even if it cost our lives. It was my responsibility to ensure it did not come to that.

I kept up a steady stream of instructions as we travelled.

"We will be expected to live human, which means dry. Whilst we are at the islands, I will remain in my human form for the duration. You may swim, but only after dark and where the humans cannot see you. You may eat as you please, but when humans are present, we will eat what and as they do. We must keep a supply of human food, just in case. We all have our preferences; it will be important that we keep those on

hand.

"Our strength and agility are greater than theirs, for we require these more than they do. They have grown soft whilst we have not. We must take care that this is not too apparent. This is unlikely to be difficult, but still we must take care.

"Our vision and hearing are more perceptive than that of humans; we must also take care that they do not discover this.

"We must use human names and human language whilst in their hearing and sight. I will be Vanessa, Maria will retain her name and Apalala must use Belinda once more. Our human names and human speech must be unremarkable and ordinary.

"Under no circumstances do we sing above water. The humans react peculiarly to this, particularly the males. Singing is, of course, permissible beneath the water's surface. We may need this to call fish or other creatures.

"Human drinks will also be necessary. This will include a reasonable quantity of alcohol, which must be consumed carefully, so we do not make mistakes.

"We must wear human clothing at all times, or at least when visible to them. I recommend we choose only one or two colours each and restrict our purchases to

these colours, so we do not mix them up.

"We must associate with humans and appear human, which means being as polite as possible, without being too friendly or antagonistic.

"Humans value privacy, with walls they can hide behind. This will work to our advantage, if we can remember this, for it means we can be out of sight and this will not draw their attention as it would among our kind.

"We do not shape water or waves where they may be perceived by humans, unless it is absolutely necessary.

"We will first go to the islands off the coast, where there is a fishing settlement. We shall remain there and fish from a boat as they do, for the duration of the fishing season. We will obtain as much information as we can from the humans at the fishing settlement, before we relocate to the nearest city. If further information is required…"

Apalala was the most vocal of my daughters, so she was the first to interrupt my flow. *"Sirena, is there no end to your advice? We have lived dry among humans before."*

I remembered well her last time on land, for I had been there, too. I reminded myself to use her human name, Belinda, even in my thoughts. *"But not for this long. And you must remember that I cannot use my name until I return to the water once more. Even in your thoughts I must be Vanessa."*

Belinda's curiosity persisted. *"Why did you choose Vanessa? It is not similar to your name — it does not even have a similar meaning."*

"Vanessa is the name of a character in a moving picture for human children. An old witch, who lives in the ocean, transforms herself into a beautiful human woman to seduce a human man. The name she takes as a human is Vanessa," I tried to explain. When I had first heard of it, I had been using my real name on land, but I had known that I would need a new one to ensure my ageless appearance went unremarked upon.

Maria broke her silence to give voice to her shock. *"Do you plan to seduce a human man, in addition to our duty here?"*

Both Belinda and I considered her sister's words amusing. I found the idea intriguing, but unlikely. *"Not at present. However, as I may not swim in the evenings, I will need to find something to occupy my time. Perhaps I will purchase some books."*

Maria interrupted my thoughts with more

practical considerations. *"First we must reach the land. How long will it be?"*

Both girls were adults, yet their impatience to reach our destination mirrored that of human children. I smiled, but replied in a more serious vein. *"We should reach the islands soon after dark. We can rest there for a time and continue to the mainland at dawn. Then we can fit out our vessel and return with it to the islands."*

Belinda's smile remained. *"Then come, Vanessa, shift your venerable tail so we may spend our first night in human beds and not on the seabed!"*

The seabed was rising and the water was lightening. It wasn't long before we could hear the boom of surf above on the reefs. I guided them through the passages and we surfaced. Fractured moonlight on the water was the only sign of the reefs on the surface, part of the islands' curse. Amid all the contrasts, this remained unchanged.

The water was dark, as was the island we approached, for the fishing season had not yet started. I lifted my head and said the words in the humans' language, "Welcome to the Houtman Abrolhos Islands, girls. They may be cursed, but for a time they will also be home."

JOE

"The Abrolhos is cursed, with murder, mutiny and lust," the pilot said suddenly, as the mist on the water resolved into some very flat islands. The tourists were glued to their windows, craning for a look. "On a stormy night almost 400 years ago, the Dutch ship *Batavia* was sailing from the Cape of Good Hope to Batavia in Indonesia. The lookout saw what he thought was moonlight on the water, but it was foam of the breakers on Morning Reef. The ship struck the reef just there..." The pilot banked the plane as we passed the reef, so he could pass over it again for the tourists on the other side of the plane.

"You can just see where the ship sank. The waves kept pushing that ship until it carved a hole in the reef, where divers found it around 50 years ago...they brought the ship up and put it in the Museum in Fremantle, leaving that blue boat-shaped hole in the reef..."

The Abrolhos Air Charter pilot continued, giving details about murders, mutiny, executions, and some hero called Wiebbe Hayes, whose heroism seemed dependent on a lot of luck. I wasn't clear on where mutiny came in, but the lust involved either some women or the treasure that had been on the ship. Maybe both.

I looked at the little wave-shaped island where all the horrors had happened, with a few buildings huddled together on it. *A few weeks marooned on that sandbar and I'd go mad, too. I hope Dean hasn't sent me to an even smaller pile of sand surrounded by ocean. If he has, I'll report him for the Playboy centrefolds he sticks on the ceiling of the ute, every time we leave civilisation.*

The plane flew over a much larger island, with an orange gravel airstrip that stood out against the white limestone and grey-green shrubs. There were even fewer buildings on this island than tiny, wave-shaped Beacon Island. At the northern end, a beautiful white beach stretched its arms around blue-green water. A couple of yachts were moored in the bay. *Wow, what I'd give to be able to afford to do that. I wonder if my island has a beach that good? I'll buy Dean a beer if it does.*

The plane veered north now, across multicoloured waters in blue and green between the brown reefs, toward the island at the northern end of the Abrolhos. "North Island approach..." the pilot intoned, turning sharply to point the plane south.

North Island was a big sand island, with a lake at the north. Houses were clustered in the south east corner of the island. Coming in to land, I realised the gravel airstrip looked really close and really, really short.

I didn't have time to panic before the wheels touched the gravel, more gently than any jet landing at an airport. The plane taxied up next to a rusted shed. A plank was hanging on the front of it, which some comedian had painted with the words, "North Island

International Airport." A man was standing beside the shed, next to a quad bike with a shiny aluminium trailer. It had to be aluminium. Anything else would rust in the salt.

One man unbuckled his seatbelt and climbed out of the plane. The pilot helped the guy unload his gear onto the gravel, before he got back in the plane and prepared to take off again.

We took off south over the buildings. I saw the two men load their gear into the quad bike trailer before they headed through the dunes to the settlement. The pilot started telling the tourists about the fishing industry, as we left North Island and flew toward West Wallabi.

He flew low over West Wallabi, telling us about how Weibbe Hayes had fought off the mutineers from a building that you could still see on the ground. I saw the outline of some square limestone walls as we flew over. I shrugged. Old shipwrecks had little appeal to me. *They're all long dead now, whoever they were and whatever they did.*

The island gave way to ocean again and I

could see more inhabited islands, like squashed sea urchins or some kind of exotic bacteria, with jetties sticking out at all angles from the two islands. The pilot mentioned something about pigeons and lobsters and I tuned out again.

I looked down at the islands. These were covered in houses, almost as dense as suburbs in the mainland. Would my island home be like that – with neighbours that would complain every time I flushed the toilet or played music? *I bet I'm next door to the oldest, grumpiest fisherman. A bloke who hates the slightest noise, but has his radio and TV on so loud I can hear the actors breathing from next door. And his toilet will be closest to my place, so I hear his every fart.*

The islands were gone and we were flying over ocean again, headed toward the next group of islands. I had a map, but I couldn't remember the name of the island I was landing on, or even the group. *Maybe it will come as a nice surprise. Maybe there will be palm trees.* I crossed my fingers for a nice white beach.

"Why is it called the Easter Group?" one of the tourists asked into his headset.

"I dunno," the pilot said.

Probably the explorers who named it had run out of names and they were here at Easter, so they figured that would do. I looked out the window, to see if any of the islands were shaped like sheep, rabbits or Easter eggs. *Nope.*

"That one is Rat Island and I know why it's called that. Apparently it was infested with them." The pilot sounded really pleased at this. "We'll be landing briefly there to drop off one of the rock lobster fishers and then we'll head out over the Pelsaert Group."

I looked around and realised the fisher he was talking about was me. *Rat Island? Dean, you bastard, you've sent me to an island infested with rats? I'm going to catch some and add those to your swag on the first night…*

"I'll show you where the *Zeewijk* was wrecked in 1727. They built themselves a new boat out of the wreckage and sailed it to Indonesia…" the pilot continued, oblivious to my seething.

Hell, if I was wrecked on one of these islands, I'd take up carpentry real fast, too.

One island was approaching really fast and

really low. The gravel of another airstrip was dead ahead and it seemed to end in the water. The water looked real close...*OH SHIT. We're going to go off the end of the runway and into the water!*

BELINDA

"We are almost out of human food, so it is time for another supply run. You will both take the carrier boat to Geraldton, replenish our food and fuel supplies, and return to the islands with the carrier boat." Vanessa's peremptory tone was no different on land or in the water.

I felt a momentary desire for rebellion as I responded. *"You mean you are almost out of ice cream?"*

I laughed at her frown, for I knew I was correct. I turned away and began washing the dishes in the sink.

I heard Vanessa's voice reply. *"I have no ice cream, no fruit, no sugar, no bread and nothing to drink but beer and water. Oh, and some milk. It has been four weeks. I cannot swim and so I cannot fish; I must have human food to maintain my reputation as a human. Do you not also have limited supplies?"*

I regretted my hasty words. She played a far more difficult part than we did, for she was more visible to the humans. Remaining on board the vessel with limited contact with humans, we could live more normally than she did, but it had its drawbacks, too. *"We fish often. If you wish, we will bring extra fish home for you, as you cannot catch your own. Nevertheless, we are out of chilli and low on coffee and chocolate. I would like to obtain more of that human liquor that burns..."* I broke off, tempted by the thought of whiskey.

Vanessa's frown lifted as I warmed to the thought of time on the mainland. Her tone softened, too. *"If you are referring to the burning drink you prefer, the humans call it whiskey. You will undertake a full, complete supply run?"*

Maria responded before I could. Her tone was businesslike. *"Yes, we will go shopping. We will bring back all the things we are short on and some more alcohol for Belinda. When does the carrier boat leave?"*

"It departs in two days, in the early morning, returning two days after that. I trust that will be enough time to complete your shopping?" Vanessa's manner was calmer than the water's surface outside.

I concentrated carefully on scrubbing a cup.

Maria eyed me as she spoke. *"As long as Belinda does not feel she needs new clothing, the time will be sufficient."*

I stuck my tongue out at Maria, but retracted it before making a peace offering to Vanessa. I did not want to jeopardise my chances of obtaining more whiskey by bad behaviour. *"We will fish for you tonight and tomorrow. I will see if I can find you a sweet little shark or a groper. I know you are partial to those."*

JOE

When the plane landed safely on the airstrip, to my stunned amazement, there were three people waiting in a shed at the edge of the gravel. I helped the pilot pull my bags out and drop them on the gravel, then shouldered my backpack and other bag and looked around. The other two guys headed off down the track next to the shed, toward the buildings on the east coast of the island. I watched them, unsure.

The remaining man in the shed came over to me. "You must be Joe Fisher, Dean's friend. I'm Skipper Hartog. You can call me Skipper. Everyone else does." He reached out to shake my hand.

His shake was firm and calloused, which made me worry my hands would feel too soft to him, like I was too soft for this work. *I've worked for months out at remote sites, sleeping in a tent and cooking outside. I've had to shake my sleeping bag out every night to make sure nothing else was alive in it and if I forgot to zip my swag up properly I was guaranteed not to wake up alone. Sometimes I couldn't have a wash because there were crocodiles in the bloody river. This bloke goes fishing every day. How hard can it be?*

He led the way down the track, keeping up a commentary over his shoulder as he went.

"You get your own deckie's camp, down by my jetty. It used to be my Dad's main camp, till we built the big one I'm in now." He pointed at a bright orange building, between us and the ocean. "There's food in the fridge; if you want anything else or you run out of something, let me know and we'll get it shipped over in the next week or two, on the carrier boat. Your water is rainwater – keep your showers and washing short, or you'll run out and then you'll have to pay to bring it over from the mainland, or have cold, salt showers.

"You'll have your own dinghy to use. It's my spare, but it's always been the deckie's dinghy, so you can go fishing or visiting at the other islands if you want. There's a club on Little Rat." He pointed vaguely south. "We buy some beer through the Co-Op and have a few evenings there in the season, especially when there's bad weather and no fishing the next day."

He stopped in front of the door of a boxy old asbestos donga, painted the same eye-watering shade of orange as the other house to the north. He unlocked the door and swung it open, leaving the key in. "This is your place. Power's off my generator, so if your lights go out, come and bang on my door and I'll take a look."

I frowned. "I'm a licensed electrician. I can fix a generator."

He looked thoughtful. "Dean did say you were a sparky, but he made you sound like Superman, too, 'cause he's full of shit sometimes. Well, if you want to do some electrical work for me or the other fishers after we're done fishing for the day, go ahead. You can probably get some good cash jobs that way, because it's cheaper than flying a sparky over from Gero. You've got to be better than the last deckie Dean recommended – he got drunk and stumbled off a cliff, right at the beginning of the season. Dumb as a box of hammers, that one.

"We're a pretty good bunch over here, a good community. We take care of each other and try not to piss each other off. Keep the noise down, be nice to your neighbours and you should be okay.

"Oh, and one more thing – all the women out here are pretty tough, all from fishing families. Don't mess with them."

I snorted. "Or I'll be dealing with big fishing dads, brothers and husbands?"

He almost smiled. "Something like that."

He continued along the track, which changed from rock and concrete to white pieces of dead coral. "Stick to the paths and tracks, take a torch when you're walking at night. There, that's my occupational health and safety responsibility done. You'll want an early night, because we start before the sun's up. I'll show you the ropes tomorrow. I'll come bang on your door when it's time to get up."

He disappeared from view around the next house, his steps on the coral bits sounding like someone sweeping up broken glass.

I went into the donga with my bags. Inside, there was a tiny little kitchen with a wonky kitchen table and four mismatched chairs. There was a wall that ran most of the way across the donga, with a gap near one end. I took a step through the gap, to find a bedroom with two double bunks, one on either side. A doorway at the other end of the room led to a boxy little bathroom, with a shower and a basin.

Where's the toilet? I wondered.

I dumped my bags on the floor between the bunks and went back into the kitchen. I looked out through the salt-encrusted window to see an old dunny, down a path outside. *Well, the bedroom's bigger than my swag and there's a flushing toilet. That beats digging a hole when you don't want to bother with one of those chemical bucket toilets.*

I looked around the kitchen. There was a

tiny, boxy TV on top of the very old fridge, with a vintage VCR that looked about as old as I was. It was held together with brown sticky tape. There was a stack of recorded videos next to it. I took a look at the handwritten labels.

They all seemed to be holiday videos, from someone called Debbie who went to the US. *Debbie does Dallas, Debbie does Iowa, Debbie does college...it looks like Debbie really liked Dallas, because there's three videos with that name, all numbered.* I stuck one of them in the VCR and turned the TV on. I hit play and opened up the fridge.

Nice, beer. There was half a case of beer in the fridge, varying from good stuff to a few odd ones that I'd never seen before. Swan Gold? The logo looked like something my Dad drank when I was a kid. *I wonder how long it's been here?*

I put the retro beer back in the fridge. In with the beer, I had some random sauce bottles, salad dressing and an unopened carton of long-life milk. *Where's the food?*

I opened up the freezer. Frozen meals,

steaks, frozen vegies, a loaf of bread and some sausages, all of them encased in the ice coating the inside of the freezer. I managed to free up a box so encrusted in ice I couldn't read the label. I knocked some of the ice off and recognised a picture of lasagne. *Dinner.*

I looked around for a microwave, but came up blank. *I wonder if you can cook these things in the oven?* I bashed some more of the ice off into the sink until I could see the instructions on the back. *Yeah, you can do frozen meals in the oven, without a microwave. Who would have guessed?*

I could hear weird noises. *Hell, it sounds like the neighbours are having sex, so loud I can hear it next door.*

I went outside to see if I could work out who my noisy neighbours were, but I couldn't hear anything from out there. I went back in.

*Yep, I can still hear them in her*e. I looked around and the little TV screen caught my eye. It looked like while Debbie was in Dallas, she saw more action than I ever got. I watched it for a few minutes, not taking my eyes off the screen as I groped around for the remote control. Eventually, I found it and pressed the fast-forward button on the VCR. By the time I'd fast forwarded to the credits at the end, I felt like a real idiot.

Ah, shit. They're all dodgy copies of old porn films. I bet Dean's stayed here, watched them all and told me about them in detail at night on site. Nothing to do at night here, either.

BELINDA

"The humans here only notice the changes to fish and weather, yet the most experienced among them express their fear of change. They somehow feel that change is coming and they are unsure of what it will mean, fearing that the change will be significant for their lives and livelihood. Yet their concept of change is nebulous and not defined. They seem to accept me now, however. I shall ask more of them as time progresses. I still need access to outside communication. This will necessitate further trips to the mainland if communication remains limited here." Vanessa looked worried as she said it.

All three of us considered her summary, seated around the table in the main cabin of the vessel. There was good reason why the local humans accepted her, but as long as Maria and I remained aboard the vessel and avoided the humans, we would not blend as well with their community. Still, if she sent us to the mainland to glean information from computers, we would stand out far more than we did here.

Maria voiced my own thoughts. *"Our knowledge of human computer technology is limited. No one else could undertake this but you."*

Vanessa's smile was rueful. Perhaps she, too, had been thinking in a similar vein to me. *"Yet I am the most accepted on the land, here, too. I cannot be in two places at once. If communication were improved here, I could use the technology to search for information from the islands, in the afternoons and evenings once my fishing duties are complete. Whilst you swim, don't forget to listen to the humans on land. They may confide in each other what they do not speak of to us."*

The sound of a footfall on the coral shingle had us all looking toward the land. A human had moved onto the coral path.

"There is a human outside your land house,

Vanessa. It appears that he is a new deckhand for the Dolphin to replace the one who was injured," I remarked.

Maria's words were as dark as the shirt she removed as she glared at the new human. *"I hope this one has better manners."*

"He certainly has a physique which is more pleasing to the eye. His upper body musculature is well defined and his rear is particularly shapely." Vanessa was thoughtful.

I tried not to laugh. "A cute bum and big muscles don't say anything about his manners, Vanessa." Sometimes human words were more expressive, particularly when using the vernacular to describe human anatomy.

"I didn't say he had a cute bum, Belinda." She inclined her head, clearly evaluating him. "I would say he has a damn fine arse."

All three of us laughed. Nothing was as funny as one of our people admiring a human, for it was so unlikely. Humans were a source of information or products. They produced what we needed and were used accordingly; contact was as limited as necessary to ensure our people remained hidden from them.

I started to remove my clothing in preparation for a night-time swim.

Vanessa gathered her choice of fish. *"I will go and speak with him, so that I may examine him more closely."* She took one fish in each hand and started down the jetty toward the human.

Maria and I slid over the side of the vessel and sank into the water, watching.

I kept my voice low as I addressed my comment to Maria. *"Why do I feel this new human means trouble for us all?"*

JOE

After dinner, I sat on the veranda in a chair made of old craypots and cracked open a beer.

It was almost dark, so I could only dimly make out the outlines of the row of jetties in the anchorage. *For all its isolation, the Abrolhos are bloody noisy,* I thought. The birds were peeping and wailing, the wind was whistling around the big Fisheries camp in the middle of the island and rattling a metal roller door that I wished someone would fix. The generators buzzed like air conditioners on a hot night in Hedland. The waves came from the south, rolling through the anchorage and lapping at boats and jetties alike.

I heard squeaky chattering, like dolphins, and a splash. Then another. I got up and walked to the edge of the cliff, peering out across the anchorage. Did dolphins come out at night?

I drank my beer, scanning the water for any sign of them. I turned my head at another squeak and splash, but still I saw nothing. I finished up the beer and threw the empty out over the water, where I thought the sounds had come from.

I caught movement in the corner of my eye and turned, hoping to catch a glimpse of something. Out of the darkness came a tall woman. Her hair hung down her back, almost to her waist, framing what looked like perfect curves. I felt like a teenager again, when I'd been mesmerised by Pamela Anderson's boobs bouncing along the beach in *Baywatch*. As she walked along the path, coming closer, I saw that her perfect curves included an incredible pair of breasts that wouldn't have looked out of place on *Baywatch*. Her long hair was blonde and, in keeping with the *Baywatch* theme, what I could see of her skin was lightly tanned and smooth. She wore a fitted blue t-shirt, the colour of the ocean on a cloudy day, and a little pair of denim shorts that exposed most of her shapely legs. In each hand, she held a fish by the gills. One was a small shark, the other some sort of fish with a white chin and fangs.

I dimly heard something clunk near my feet, but all my attention was fixated on the approaching vision.

I swallowed a couple of times before I could speak. "Been fishing?" I asked her, my voice coming out hoarse.

"My deckhands have been, and they know he's my favourite." She held up the fanged fish.

"What is that?" I asked. *Don't tell me it's a vampire fish, and that's why you like it. My little sisters would.*

She laughed, a pleasant sound. "He's a baldchin groper, possibly one of the tastiest fish in the sea, after tuna and wahoo, of course."

*I'd like to grope her one day. As for wahoo…*I shook my head – that had to be the beer talking.

She was less than two metres away from me now and I saw she was the same height as me. Her face was open and pretty; her smile infectious.

She stuck both fish under one arm and knelt down in front of me. I froze in panic. She picked something up from near my feet and slowly straightened up, close enough to touch if I'd had the guts to lift my hand. Her eyes were stormy blue – the same colour as her shirt – and they were laughing.

"Have you been playing with the dolphins?" she admonished, holding up what I recognised as the beer bottle I'd thrown into the water. It was now dripping wet, half full of seawater. I took it from her, wordlessly. "You shouldn't do that. They throw things back. You're lucky it didn't hit you and only landed by your feet."

She looked out across the dark water, frowning. I heard squeaking and a big splash, then nothing.

"I'm Giuseppe. Joe. Joe Fisher," I managed to say, sticking out a hand in the faint hope she'd shake mine. "Deckhand on...whatever boat Skipper Hartog has."

She turned back to me. When she took my hand, hers was cool and firm. The frown vanished, replaced by a friendly smile. "Ah, the new deckhand on the *Dolphin*. I hope you'll be better than your predecessor, not that it'll take much. I'm Vanessa, skipper on the *Siren*, and your next-door neighbour." She waved at the house beside mine, painted to match her shirt.

Oh my God, I don't live next door to a grumpy, flatulent old man. Instead, I get the hottest woman I've ever seen in the flesh for a neighbour. "So I should come to you if I need to borrow a cup of sugar?" I asked hopefully.

"I think I'm out of sugar." Her tone was slightly less friendly as she frowned again. "Milk or coffee I may be able to assist you with." She took a deep breath. "As long as you don't feel the need to have any wild, drunken parties, we should get along fine. Or I'll set the dolphins on you." She smiled at me again, her voice light with laughter. She winked, then turned and went into her blue house.

I was left staring after her. *I think I'm in love.* I was already wondering how to throw a wild, drunken party so she'd come over to complain.

Maybe even in a nightdress with no bra…

"Did you manage dinner all right?" Skipper's voice came out of the darkness, as he came up the path behind me.

I turned to face him. "Dinner's fine," I managed to say. "I just met…" I looked toward her blue house, unable to articulate her name.

He laughed. "You met Vanessa."

"She seemed really nice," I stammered.

"Yeah, she can," he said darkly. "Look, the best advice I can give you is to stay away from her."

My heart fell. "Let me guess, she has a father and brothers who are all pro-wrestlers and her husband is a prize fighter?"

Skipper laughed again, but there was an edge to it. "No, Vanessa got her fishing licence from her mother, who died a few years ago. Now her mother, Serena, was one beautiful woman." He paused, evidently remembering. "And Vanessa looks just like her. She's got two deckies, who might not balk at taking a swing at you, but not pro-wrestlers or prize fighters, either of them."

"Then she's married to the Incredible Hulk?" I suggested.

"Nah mate, Vanessa's not married, and I don't think she wants to be." He hesitated. "Look, just stay away from her and don't piss her off."

Or she'll set the dolphins on me.

"Sure." I shrugged. "Well, good night. See you in the morning."

BELINDA

Maria headed into deeper water, whilst I ventured closer to the island. It was too dark for the human to see me, so I kept my head above the surface to hear their conversation.

The human didn't notice her at first. He was looking in my direction, though I knew I was invisible to him. He threw the brown glass bottle in his hands at me, but it fell short. The bottle started to fill with seawater and sank in front of me. Angry at his careless action, I lifted the bottle from the water and waited for his attention to be elsewhere. I was going to throw the bottle back at him and knock him out.

Vanessa saw me and gave the slightest shake of her head. I dropped the bottle back into the water, where it bobbed in the waves, half submerged. This gave me an idea.

He turned to look at her, too tongue-tied to offer even a proper greeting. Stupid human.

I felt the power of the little waves, not strong enough to wet the cliff top. I pushed one wave into another, shaping it under the bottle to carry it up to the top of the low cliff. My wave crested the cliff, sending the bottle and a wash of water over the stupid human's feet.

He did not notice. He was gaping at her.

She noticed. She lifted the bottle up and turned her unhappy expression in my direction.

"If the human ceases throwing his waste at me, I will not throw any more back at him," I told her in our language, barely perceptible to humans above the water.

And with this, I turned tail, letting my flukes splash in the shallow water, heading into deeper water to find some dolphins to play with.

JOE

It was still dark when the pounding started on my door. I didn't know where I was and it took me a minute to work out how to turn on the light and open the front door.

"Get a shirt on. It's time for work," Skipper told me, as he turned away to head down his jetty.

I grabbed the nearest shirt and stepped into my rubber thongs. I put the shirt on as I followed him down the jetty.

My first morning fishing was an unmitigated disaster.

I looked for buoys in the water when Skipper told me to, but I couldn't see in the pitch dark. He always ended up spotting them. Then I had to hook the rope up to the winch, which pulled the craypot (a big, slotted box around a metre to a side and maybe half that high) out of the water. When I opened the pot, all the lobsters fell out. I learned that if I didn't have the tub in place just right, then they spilled out onto the deck, snapping like a pack of crocodiles.

I picked one up, looking for claws that just didn't seem to be there, and felt something close over my toe with a snap. I looked down to find one of the bastards had clamped its tail on my toe. I dropped the one I was holding into the tub and tried to shake its mate off my foot. When Skipper finally pulled the bastard off me, he measured it up, said, "Nah, she's too small," and threw her over the side.

My toe was bleeding and it felt like it was broken. *Bitch,* I thought. *Wish I'd brought my steel-capped boots.*

"Get a band aid on that before you start attracting sharks. First aid kit's in the cabin, with the life jackets," Skipper ordered, throwing lobsters rapidly from the deck into the tub, never missing.

It took me ages to find the first aid kit. It was buried underneath the life jackets and a nest of ropes, in a cabin that looked like the shed of some kind of hoarder boatie.

My toe still hurt like hell as I limped back on deck. "What next?"

I want to go back to bed.

I saw stars as something hit me in the face. The stench hit me next.

"Get out the way or you'll get a rotten cray in the face," Skipper shouted.

I looked down at the rotting remains of a lobster on the deck. Bits of it were still on the shoulder of my shirt.

"Don't just stand there. Bait the pot up and drop it back over the side." Skipper sounded even more annoyed.

Still covered in rotten lobster, I grabbed some fish heads and stuffed them into the craypot.

I couldn't bait a pot to save my life. I put too much in, I put them in the wrong place, I didn't put enough in, or I forgot to bait the pots up at all before I dropped them over the side. Then I had to winch them up and try again.

Another of the lobster bitches clipped my finger with her tail. It wasn't broken, but it still bled, so I was sent back into the cabin for the first aid kit. Every pot after that, my hand stung like hell from the salt water. The only good thing about it was that it kept me awake.

I got hit by another flying dead lobster, this time in the stomach. It was so far gone that it splattered. The stench was unbelievable. *Maybe Skipper'll smell me coming in the dark, so he won't throw another one at me.*

I wanted breakfast, I wanted to go back to bed and most of all, I wanted a shower. *Fuck fishing. I want to go home.*

I barely noticed the sun coming up, until I realised I could see Skipper's face clearly in the daylight. He was steering the boat back to Rat Island, not saying a word to me.

I helped him tie up at the jetty and climbed off the boat dejectedly.

"Hey, Joe," Skipper called after me.

I turned, not really interested in how bad a deckie he thought I was, but it was too ingrained in me not to be rude if I could avoid it.

"Not bad for a first day," Skipper said. "We got a fair catch. You're faster than the last bloke I had. Go grab some breakfast and I'll see you again, same time tomorrow."

I have to do this again? Fuck. Dean is not going to know a night of peace, he'll be sleeping with spiders for the next MONTH.

I nodded vaguely in his direction and dragged myself down the jetty back to my veranda.

"Good morning. How was your first day fishing?" a friendly female voice called.

Sitting on her veranda, her hair a glowing gold in the watery early morning sunlight, was Vanessa. She sipped from a steaming cup in her hand, her knees bent up and to one side. In her shorts and singlet, she looked like she was posing for a photo shoot on beach house holidays. *Fishing might be worth it if I get greeted by a sight like this at the end of every trip.*

Shit, I wanted to tell her, but I couldn't bring myself to say it aloud. I struggled to find a way to make it sound like I wasn't the most useless deckie ever.

"Did Skipper tell you that you'd be more useful as cray bait than as a deckie?" She looked like she was trying not to laugh.

I shook my head, annoyed, and found my voice. "No. We had a good catch today. He told me I wasn't bad and I was better than the last bloke."

"From him, that's high praise, then. But you still had a run in with a few crays." She laughed. "You've got rotten cray guts all over your shirt, I can smell it from here. Ugh, don't get any closer until you've had a shower."

I stumbled up the steps to my veranda, eager for a hot shower.

I shut the door behind me and staggered toward the tiny bathroom. I dropped my daks on the concrete of the bunkroom floor and grabbed a threadbare towel from the hook on the wall.

I hung the towel over the bathroom door and squeezed inside. I turned the water on in the shower and waited for it to heat up.

I heard voices outside, close enough to make out every word.

"So, how bad is your new deckie, Skipper?" Vanessa asked sympathetically.

The bathroom window must be right next to her veranda, I thought.

"He's not as bad as the last bloke. He didn't drop any of our catch over the side, he didn't fall in and he didn't fall asleep. He might end up being a good deckie, if he doesn't do anything stupid so he ends up in hospital."

The shower's taking forever to warm up, I thought impatiently.

Vanessa sounded serious. "Did you give him the safety talk, like I told you?"

Vanessa's the local safety rep? Shit, I better wear my steel-capped boots tomorrow, so she notices I work safe.

"Yeah, I did. I can't afford to lose another deckie this season. I'm behind already." Skipper sounded grumpy. His tone changed. "So what did you think of him?"

"Well, if he's as quick to learn as you say, he might last out the season. He doesn't seem as stupid as the last one. Maybe…" Vanessa tailed off, without finishing her sentence.

Skipper cleared his throat. "He still has a

fair bit to learn, though. He's good for target practice when he gets confused."

Vanessa laughed. "Did you have to throw the rotten crays at him?"

I heard Skipper laugh. "The first one was an accident, he got in the way. The second one...well, he was already wearing one and he looked like he might fall asleep. I figured the smell might wake him up a bit."

"You know, you'll need to replace those gas bottles. He'll need hot water to wash the smell off. A cold shower won't cut it." Vanessa had stopped laughing.

"Yeah, I got some coming over on the carrier boat tomorrow," Skipper said. "A couple of days of cold showers won't hurt him."

No hot water? Shit! I stepped into the water. *Oh, it's fucking cold, too! Give me a river with crocs in it. At least those rivers were warm.*

BELINDA

"Can you remember which ice cream she prefers? I cannot recall and the stuff comes in so many colours!" For the first time, Maria looked flustered.

I tried to assist. *"Try blue. Is there a blue?"*

"There is blue packaging, but no blue product." Her voice crept louder, but there were no humans nearby to hear her.

I scanned the cold cabinet with the glass doors, before pointing to my recommendation. *"This one is pink and features a picture of berries. She likes berries. This will suffice."*

Maria lost interest in the ice cream and turned to the cold shelves on her other side. *"I would like to try this coffee milk. It appears to be cold* and contains coffee. *I will not burn my tongue with this.*"

I looked at the list Vanessa had given us, as we wheeled the metal trolley between the aisles of products. "*She will want meat, like the humans eat. They do not just eat fish, so she must do the same.*"

Maria examined the products on either side of us, until one caught her eye. "*She also likes these fungus items. Look, there is a flat bread meal with pieces of fungus on top. Which will she prefer?*"

The products she indicated were round, flat and yellow, sprinkled with other materials. They all looked much alike.

"*We are here to purchase food for several weeks. I recommend we purchase some of each. If we need food for several weeks, fresh is not sufficient. We must purchase more of what will preserve for longer. Items which are frozen or encased in metal will remain fresh for longer. Those fruits are frozen. We should purchase more of those.*" I directed Maria's attention to the fruit and she looked at them thoughtfully.

"*She has expressed a preference for berries. What are these orange items? Mango cheeks? I thought mango was a fruit. Aren't cheeks a body part?*"

I patted my face, then reconsidered and

touched my behind, too.

"They might be pieces from the rump of the fruit? She will not approve and I will not touch them."

I almost agreed with her, but a sudden thought made me return to the box of strangely named fruit. *"She may approve. She expressed her preference for that male human's rump. Perhaps her taste runs to these? I will purchase some and explain my reasoning if she complains."* I suppressed my laughter at the thought.

I need not have worried, for Maria's attention was caught by another package of food. *"Moon-shaped pastries? These look interesting. I will purchase these also."*

In another aisle, I looked for the last item on the list, something with which to restrain hair. I found round, stretchy fabric rings and shiny, flat fabric strips on a cardboard roll. The rings came in blue, but the strips were only available in pink and yellow. Thinking of the ice cream, I chose the pink. I placed several packets of the blue rings and the pink strips into the trolley, hoping these would suffice.

We paid for our purchases, once we had completed our selection. Maria packed the items into white foam boxes for storage and transport in the back of our vehicle. I returned the wheeled trolley. In the window of another shop, some human swimwear caught my eye. A picture displayed near them showed a human woman wearing this swimwear, lying down on a beach in the bright sunlight.

I reflected that I would like to recline on a beach one day. If this was appropriate attire, then I had to obtain some.

I ventured into the shop. The swimwear was pale blue, the colour of Vanessa's clothing, but if these were required, I would make sure I conformed to even the colour. Vanessa would understand.

But if she did not…

I purchased two sets of swim clothing, one in her size and one in mine, before I returned to the vehicle, where Maria waited impatiently.

I opened the vehicle door before I remembered an important omission. *"Oh! I forgot to purchase that fire drink!"*

Maria's impatience increased as I returned to the shop to purchase more of the drink called whiskey.

JOE

The next day was better. I set an alarm, so I'd managed to put a shirt on and drink half a coffee before Skipper started banging down my door. I pulled on my steel-capped boots before I left. *That'll keep the bitches off my toes*, I thought.

I learned that wearing steel-capped boots on a boat was tantamount to suicide, because it was like having your feet encased in concrete if you ended up in the water. Skipper offered to throw me over the side if I didn't believe him, promising me I'd sink like a rock. I worked in bare feet that day; I was back wearing rubber thongs on my feet the next day.

If you get the tub under the pot just right, the lobsters don't fall on the deck and try to snap off your toes. If you grab them right round the middle, they can't reach to snap at your fingers, either.

I learned to stay down when he was throwing the dead and undersized ones over the side. You don't get hit if you're lower than the sides of the boat. If you leave your steel-capped boots on deck while the dead lobsters are flying, Skipper uses them for target practice. I think he got some inside my boots, but most of it splattered on the outside. I left my boots on the veranda to air out, hoping the smell would be gone by the time I needed them again.

A cold shower is a bit more bearable if you wait till evening, when the water tank has been sitting in the sun all day. Then the water isn't so freezing — it could be almost skin temperature.

One day, I managed not to get any rotten lobster on my shirt. I wasn't bleeding and Skipper had actually told me, "Good job. See you tomorrow." We were back earlier, too, so

Vanessa was just stepping out onto her veranda with her steaming mug as I hit the path.

"Good morning," I greeted her.

She shaded her eyes against the rising sun behind me and peered out.

"Oh, good morning, Joe. How was your catch this morning? I didn't smell you coming. Didn't you catch any of Skipper's dead crays today?" She was laughing as she sat down, blowing the steam from her cup toward me.

"The lobster catch wasn't too bad. All the dead ones went over the side, back in the water." I actually sounded proud about it.

"So are you sick of fishing yet, ready to tell Skipper where he can stick his crays?" she teased.

"No," I told her honestly. "It's not that bad, if you take away the early starts and the bloody lobsters with their tails. Besides, I think Skipper knows where to put his lobsters after he's caught them. He's been fishing here for years. If I tried to tell him what to do with his catch, I think I'd be on the next plane back to Geraldton. Or maybe a leaky dinghy, with no motor and a paddle if I'm lucky." I smiled. I'd also learned that Skipper's sense of humour wasn't always funny.

She looked surprised. "Hmm, Skipper could be right. You might make a good deckie."

It was my turn to be surprised. "Why stick around if I'm only going to be a bad one? There's no point in that."

I headed back into my house. It was time for breakfast.

BELINDA

Our hotel was near the water, but we chose to eat human food instead of taking a swim to catch our own. The port seemed too busy, with too many lights, to creep naked into the water unseen.

We chose a restaurant at random. We both ordered chilli mussels with beer to drink. Our tastes differed in many things, as much as our appearances, but Maria and I both had a taste for chilli. This became problematic at the islands, as our stock rapidly became depleted, but this trip we had purchased large quantities of condiments containing chilli. I hoped we would not run out.

"Are you new here, or just passing through?" The man behind the bar who took our order sounded curious. It was apparent that we were strangers to Geraldton.

"We've been fishing out at the Houtman Abrolhos Islands, off the coast. We were sent back to Geraldton for supplies," I responded.

"A few days' fishing? Which charter boat are you on? Have you caught anything good?" The man sounded eager.

"More than a few days. We're crew from the rock lobster vessel, *Siren*. The lobster catch is not too bad this season," I replied cautiously.

"The *Siren*? I haven't heard of that boat," the man said, his expression puzzled.

A bell rang in the distance. "I'll go get your meals," he said quickly.

The chilli mussels were brought out and we ate quickly, leaving before he could ask further questions.

As Vanessa had said, we were not to be too friendly, or draw undue attention.

JOE

Later that day, the carrier boat arrived, with gas bottles for hot water, a few passengers and fresh food. It took the lobsters in their crates back to the mainland for sale.

Two of the passengers, I learned, were Vanessa's deckhands and they'd been shopping on the mainland. She sounded as excited as a five-year-old over some of their purchases.

"Ice cream!" I heard the squeal from the veranda. I stuck my head outside to take a look.

Vanessa was holding a tub of ice cream, hugging it to her chest. She looked down to read the label. "Why is it pink?"

"It's strawberry ice cream. It's supposed to be pink." The dark-haired girl sounded matter-of-fact.

Vanessa pursed her lips. "Well, I guess I'll eat it. But next time don't get the pink one. I prefer chocolate." She gave a resigned sigh and carried her ice cream into the kitchen.

I laughed quietly. One of the girls standing on Vanessa's veranda turned and saw me. The other girl turned, too.

I hurried back into my house and shut the door.

I watched them through the window, as they both carried boxes of food onto the boat tied up at the end of the jetty next to Skipper's. They didn't return, staying on board the boat.

Wow, a female skipper with girl deckies, I thought. *Who'd be happy to throw a punch at me*, I realised as I remembered Skipper's warning. I tried not to think about them as I put away my fresh supplies.

BELINDA

It was difficult to wait until dark to slip into the water again. Our time between was filled with storing our food purchases appropriately and taking Vanessa's much larger quantity of food to the house. We asked her if she would like fresh fish tonight, so that we could catch extra for her, but she declined the offer. She intended to start consuming some of the fresh human food.

The water felt cool and inviting.

Maria hesitated on the vessel, concerned. *"Should I replace the fuel supply on Vanessa's house generator before we go? It was near empty."*

I laughed, shaking my head. *"Is it difficult to*

do?"

"*No,*" Maria began thoughtfully. "*I suppose she can change the fuel lines herself if it is required before our return.*" With that, she slipped between the waves with a small splash.

There were samsonfish and kingfish in the anchorage, grown to enormous size on food scraps from the camps. We had been cautioned not to catch these, the humans' pets, and so we swam further afield. To the north east, we found tuna with yellow fins and dhufish. Algae were varied and plentiful, too. Sick of the human habit of scaling and cooking the fish, we ate the fish as our people always had, seasoned with nothing but salt water. Watching Maria with her fish, I was reminded of a human child crunching through a chocolate bar.

When we had eaten our fill, we sang up the dolphins. They had missed us, they said, and wished to play in the channel, where they had found a large school of tuna fish that morning. Perhaps some would remain as a snack after a play.

We raced the dolphins to the channel,

through reefs and around rocks and islands. It felt good to swim at full speed, to feel the power of muscle and tail flukes as we streamed through the water in what felt like a cloud of bubbles. I wondered if this was what it felt like to fly through air, but caught myself in time before my dreams flew too high. Even humans could only fly with the aid of an aircraft, which was a metal tube with wings. My sensation of speed was as little like flying in a metal tube as travelling on the carrier boat this afternoon had been like swimming: no comparison.

JOE

A bloke in shorts and a uniform shirt was loading boxes from the carrier boat into a quad bike trailer.

"I don't know when we'll get a sparky over here to install this stuff," the bloke said to the skipper of the carrier boat. "And our internet and phones are down till we do."

"What's wrong with your internet and phone?" I asked.

"I dunno," he said. "We got a sparky who came over, told us we'd need this stuff, then took a job up in the mines before we got the stuff shipped up. He says he can't install it now."

"Let me take a look," I suggested.

"The Department facilities aren't just a fishing shack. All our electrical and communications work has to be carried out by a licensed electrician. Sorry mate." The bloke turned away from me to climb onto his quad bike.

"I'm a licensed electrician, have been for almost ten years. I've been wiring up mining construction and operation camps for the last three. Electrical, communications, the works. I bet I can install it. Let me take a look. If I can't do anything with it, you can still wait till you find some sparky on the mainland to come over." I shrugged.

He turned to look at me. "Mate, what are you doing here if you earn that kind of money? No one leaves a mining job to be a deckie out here."

I laughed. "I get two months off a year, and I'm on holidays. I told one of my mates I wanted to go fishing on a charter boat. He told me about this great opportunity, getting paid to go fishing as a deckie." My expression must have said it all.

The bloke laughed. "In that case, if you want to take a look, go ahead. If you can fix our communications, give me a quote. If it's not more than the other sparky's quote, I'll hire you on the spot."

"Sure," I replied. "I'll head over now."

He buzzed off on his quad bike and I trudged along the tinkling coral shingle path behind him. Tinkle, tinkle, tinkle, FUCK. *Concrete path.* I continued on, limping on what felt like two broken toes now. I hobbled up to my shack, grabbed my tools and headed back along the path.

When I'd reached the Fisheries camp, I saw the boxes were still in the trailer. I opened one up and took a look at the parts. *It looks like a full reinstall. Shit, this is going to be easy.* The uniformed bloke came into sight, carrying a ladder.

"There you go, sparky. Knock yourself out." He laughed.

"My name's Joe," I told him. "It'll be on the quote."

"I'm Glen, Senior Operations Manager out here," he replied. "If you can get our communications failure fixed, you can come over and watch the footy with us on the big camp TV whenever you want."

"When's the next match?" I asked. I was too embarrassed to tell him I didn't know what day it was. The lobsters didn't care and I didn't have TV reception in my shack.

"Tonight. West Coast versus Richmond." Glen smirked. "But the other sparky told me it'd take him a week to get that stuff installed. So, maybe next week, mate."

I laughed. "Then the other bloke was a pretty shit electrician. I bet he'd never seen some of this stuff before and he told you a week because he had no idea what he was doing. I've spent three years installing this sort of gear. I could do it with my eyes closed. I figure I got four hours till dark. If I can get your communications working by kickoff, will you pay me whatever he quoted you?"

Glen considered for a minute. "Sure mate. Bring your own beer, though."

A week's pay for four hours' work? I'll need the beer to celebrate. I nodded and got to work.

BELINDA

We played with the dolphins through the channel, from the depths to leaping across the surface. I laughed for the sheer joy of it, after the caution and control of life on land.

I dove through the remains of vessels in the depths. One ship rested on the bottom with its masts upright, as if it might sail on the surface instead of the sea floor. Once the craft of a lobster fisherman, the lobsters had reclaimed the vessel in a peculiar revenge.

The tuna were no longer in the channel. A dolphin spotted them in the passage to the north. We proceeded up the passage between the islands in the Wallabi Group, searching for the elusive fish. We could have called them to us, but my pleasure was in the chase and the swim.

Sea lions slept on shore and sharks swam through the passage. Tiger sharks, a hammerhead, some smaller whalers and a wobbegong passed us, but none had the temerity to attempt a taste of us.

I watched the sharks, wondering if they had taken the tuna, when Maria called my name.

Pointing through the coral, she looked puzzled. *"What is that? It looks like a human artefact, but it has been in the water a long time."*

We darted between the coral gardens, eerie in the light of the full moon in the sky above. Between the coral, we came upon a corroded, coral-encrusted cannon. Nearby was a large hole carved in the reef, where something had evidently been removed.

"I think it is from one of the old shipwrecks, before there were humans on these islands. The humans removed this shipwreck to display on land."

Maria touched the corroded metal of the cannon. *"There are more of these, further to the south. Do the humans not know of them all?"*

I reflected before I responded. *"Perhaps they do not. The humans fear the waves near the reefs. The pull of the water's power, the surge in the swell during a storm, the feeling of fresh water flowing across our skin…these are pleasures for our people alone. The humans know little of such things."* My sigh sent a stream of bubbles to the surface.

Maria gave a bubbly snort. *"People who cannot revel in the simple pleasures of life? I pity the humans more than ever."*

One of the dolphins called to us over our conversation. She said they would come for us the following evening, once the sun had set.

We bade the dolphins farewell, promising to return the following night to search for the school tuna. We headed quickly in the direction of the *Siren*.

JOE

On my way home after the footy was finished, I cut across the rocky scrub to the back of my shack. Just as I reached my back door, the generator behind the house sputtered and was silent. The lights in the house next door dimmed and went out. *It must be time for bed*, I thought.

I opened the door and went in. I shut it behind me and heard another door slam. Through the window, I could see a shape heading for the generator shed with a torch, swearing loudly.

I found my torch and headed back outside, toward the generator shed.

"Useless piece of shit. Now my ice cream's going to melt. I'll get a new one sent over from the mainland tomorrow." Unmistakeably female and obviously pissed off.

I stepped into the shed doorway. "Can I help?" I offered.

Vanessa crouched over the generator, a

rusted hammer in her hand. "No. I'm going to beat the crap out of this until I feel better and I'll have a new one that works tomorrow."

Wow. Sweet, friendly Vanessa has a volcanic temper.

"You might not need to. I can probably fix it," I told her. It sounded like it had just run out of fuel.

"What, because blokes know more about generators, and having boobs makes girls useless at telling when equipment needs to be replaced?" She rose to her full height stiffly. She had the hammer raised and as she turned to glare at me, she looked as if she might consider using it on me. She was quivering with anger, the aforementioned boobs doubly so.

Those boobs may not affect your technical ability, but they're distracting me from mine.

Unable to help it, I burst out laughing, my hands up in surrender. "No, because I'm a licensed electrician and I probably know more about generators than most of the people on this island. But I'm happy to let you break your hammer on it, if you like. It's your generator."

I backed away from her.

Her lips quirked into a slight smile as she looked at me quizzically. "You think you can fix this piece of shit?"

"I'm willing to try," I began, "if you hold up the torch so I can get a good look at it."

She held up her torch, spotlighting the generator, and moved out of my way.

A quick examination of the generator told me that there didn't look to be anything seriously wrong with it. I went around the back of it and kicked the fuel drum it was connected to. It echoed hollowly. *Yep, out of fuel.*

I kicked the next fuel drum and wished I hadn't – it was full. *Fuck, those broken toes hurt like hell.* Quickly, I unhooked the empty drum and connected the fuel hose to the new drum. I tried to start the generator again. It took a few tries, until the diesel had a chance to run through it, before it settled into a healthy buzz. Behind me, the lights in her house flickered back on.

I backed out of the generator shed to stand next to her, wiping my oily hands on my shorts. "So, are you going to put the hammer down now?" I asked.

She looked in surprise at the hammer clutched in her hand, before going back into the shed and hanging it on the wall. She closed the shed door behind her as she stepped back outside.

She looked at me, her expression difficult to discern in the torchlight. "Thank you," she said in wonder, holding out her hand to shake mine.

My fingers closed over hers. *Rust and diesel, salt and lubricant.* Instead of wanting to pull away and wash my hands, I held hers for longer than necessary.

"Any time," I told her. "If you have more trouble with your generator, let me know. You know where I live." Reluctantly, I let go.

She rubbed her hands together as if she was dying to wash them, but a smile lit her face. "Come in for a second and wash your hands. I'll get you a beer – it's the least I can do. After all, you saved my ice cream."

I followed her back to her house, shaking my head. *Well this has to be the strangest house call I've had yet. At least it'll make a funny story to tell in between Dean's interminable ones.*

Silhouetted in the doorway against the light, Vanessa looked mouthwatering. *Ah, he won't believe me anyway.*

I swallowed and followed her inside.

BELINDA

"What is it that you miss most of home?"

Maria's question surprised me, but there was no hesitation in my response. *"I miss my daughter, Zerafina. I do not like to be apart from her."*

"I do not miss Estella so much. She is twelve now, learning about human culture and language so that she may better blend in with them when she does her duty among them." Maria sounded thoughtful.

I was curious. *"What do you miss, then?"*

Maria hesitated before she answered. *"I miss Cantrella. Human beds are cold, alone without her. I miss her conversation and her insight."* She gave a sigh.

I thought of the elder who was Maria's

partner. *"But she would never live on land among humans for long. She does not like them."*

Maria immediately leaped to the defence of her partner. *"She did her duty among humans who were cruel and hurt her. Would you like them if they had forced themselves inside you, without your permission?"*

"I doubt I would. I understand now why you had difficulty in doing your duty, when the time came. As Cantrella's partner, you must share her thoughts and feelings often." I attempted to sound conciliatory.

Maria was thoughtful once more. *"Yes, though not always. She dislikes dolphins, also, for reasons she cannot explain. She says that they remind her of humans. Yet I have no distaste for them — they are less like humans than we are."*

I returned to my initial question. *"Is there anything else you miss?"*

Maria closed her eyes, her response deep with yearning. *"When I wake up to find the sun shining far too bright, I miss the darkness in the deep. I dislike the sense of smell we have on land, and I miss the absence of it in the water. I miss the feel of the pull of strong currents on my body in the open ocean, for the currents are dampened by the reefs and the shallow water here. I miss feeling connected through the water to every living thing in it – the air is too thin to give me that feeling."*

An amusing idea came to me. *"And when you are in the deep, is there anything of the land that you will miss?"*

Now Maria's voice was quick and businesslike. *"Coffee, chocolate, chilli and beer. And playing with the dolphins in the shallow water, though they are not of the land."*

I smiled and said, *"I will miss my fire drink, warm food and hot showers. I will miss chilli, also. Speaking of chilli, I have an idea. What do you say to bringing our catch back to the vessel and placing chilli on it before we eat it?"*

The idea struck her as it did me. *"You mean the whole fish, eating it as our people eat it, but with the addition of chilli?"*

I was eager to try this new idea. *"Yes. It seems an intriguing idea, which I suspect will have a pleasant taste."*

Maria was more cautious. *"This is an idea I would like to try. Does the type of fish matter?"*

I dismissed details in my desire to experiment. *"No, I think we will try it with whatever we catch on the swim back. Let's see who can catch the biggest!"* I darted off into the water, Maria not far behind.

JOE

"Bathroom's this way," Vanessa told me, leading the way.

I followed her through the now well-lit house. She had vinyl and tiled floors on the concrete, instead of the bare concrete in my shack. The bathroom was old, but definitely a lot better than my tiny mouldy one. I washed my hands in a sink with a brand-new bar of soap, some liquid handwash and a nailbrush that looked too clean to touch.

It looked strangely empty for a woman's bathroom. A toothbrush, the soap and not much else, except a container of salt. I'd never seen a bathroom used by a girl which didn't have some makeup or hair products scattered around. Hell, my sisters took up so much space in our shared bathroom, when I was home I gave up putting any of my stuff in there. I just used theirs and smelt of whatever fruit-scented shampoos and soaps they'd picked. There were worse things for my arse to smell of than coconut or mango.

I dried my hands on a pristine white towel that I tried to touch as little as possible.

Vanessa sidled in behind me and started to wash her own hands, taking longer than I had. I watched her for a moment. Her fingers were long and thin, topped by nails that were surprisingly short. She didn't have any nail polish on them. I looked down. Nope, none on her toes, either. I tried to focus on her toes. They looked long and straight, like her fingers, but something about them was strange. It's not that they were any longer than anyone else's toes, just…not right. I felt dizzy and closed my eyes. All those months of no drinking on site, a six-pack of beer and I'm imagining things.

I opened my eyes to find she was right in front of me, those unadorned toes almost touching my feet. *Ten perfect toes, perfectly normal.*

She reached around me to get the towel, her arm brushing my shirt.

I realised I'd frozen in exactly the wrong spot and stepped out of her way to go to the kitchen instead. She followed me, wiping her hands on the towel as she went. She hung it on the back of one of the dining chairs, before opening the fridge.

"What sort of beer would you like?" she asked. "We have Corona and something called Cooper's that one of my deckhands likes."

I accepted a Cooper's Pale Ale as she chose a Corona, opening them both with the bottle opener on the side of the fridge. *A girl's house this may be, but the bottle opener was in the right place.*

"To the miracle man who came to help a girl in distress," Vanessa said, lifting her beer to clink it against mine. We both drank.

A thought came to her as soon as she had a mouthful of beer. She put the bottle down on the table, opening her mouth to say something, then closed it again, looking embarrassed. "Would you like to sit down, in the lounge?" She said it in a rush.

"Sure," I replied, following her to the other end of the big room. There were two metal-framed futon sofas here, which presumably earned it the title of lounge.

She perched on the edge of one as I sank back into the other, leaning right back with a sigh. Even her elderly sofas were more comfortable than the one in my shack.

"I figured everyone else would be asleep," she said. "What were you still doing up, or was I making too much noise?" This had evidently just occurred to her and she looked worried.

I shrugged. "I was watching the footy with some of the Fisheries guys and I'd just got back to my shack when I heard some pretty loud swearing. I was going to go to bed, but it sounded pretty dire. I figured I'd better go help before someone got killed."

She looked down, embarrassed. "You thought I was going to kill someone?" She put the beer to her lips.

"Well, the way you held that hammer, I figured if the generator wasn't going to get it, you might use it on me," I admitted.

She almost choked on her beer as she burst

out laughing. "So you braved the mad girl with a hammer to save a generator from a violent death at her hands, at great personal danger to yourself? You're the generator's hero!"

I'd prefer to be yours. I grinned back. "Yeah, well it wouldn't be the first time I saved a generator from death."

I told her about one night out on site, when the generator had died just as Dean started cooking dinner. He'd been holding a cook's knife and cutting up steak when the lights went out. Then I told her about fixing the communications for the Fisheries camp.

She looked impressed. "You know how to install communications for a place like this, in the middle of nowhere?" she asked in disbelief.

"Sure," I told her. "That's my job the rest of the year. I set up communications and electricity for remote mining camps. Once I get the equipment and the power set up, hooking up the satellite uplinks and the network is easy..." I continued for a bit more, until I realised I was boring her. She had that polite, glazed look I wore when my sisters talked about the merits of tampons, foundation or vampires. I remembered that I was talking to a woman who'd just threatened a generator with a hammer, because she didn't know it had run out of fuel.

"I'm sorry," I apologised. "You're very easy to talk to."

She smiled. "I'm sorry that I don't understand. Do you mean that you can set up communications for a house so that we could get the internet out here?"

"Absolutely," I replied. "The equipment is a bit pricey, but if you're willing to pay for it, I can install it in an afternoon. You wouldn't even need to get an installer from the mainland."

"How pricey?" she asked.

I named a figure that was close to my monthly paycheck when I'd been installing lights back in Perth.

She nodded, thoughtfully. "And how much for you to install it?"

I told her how much the Fisheries guys had agreed to pay.

Another nod. "How soon can you order the equipment?"

"As soon as I can get to a phone. It might take a few weeks to get it out here, though," I replied. *Shit, if she pays what the Fisheries blokes did, I'll have earned two weeks' pay in a day. If every job out here pays like this, I'll have my house in one year instead of two.*

She took a deep breath. *She's just realised that I'm asking her for a lot of money.* She exhaled slowly and surprised me. "Okay. Order the lot and I'll have your money in cash, when the girls next go out on the carrier boat. I'll even make you dinner."

I opened my mouth to accept her offer, but she cut me off, blushing. "But not tonight. It's a bit late and we both have pots to pull in a few hours. Let me know when you're free." She stood up and so did I.

I headed for the front door, then went through it and across the veranda. Before I stepped out of the path of light streaming from her front door to the steps, I turned around. "Thanks. Good luck with your generator. And don't forget, if you need an electrician, I'm just next door."

I tripped lightly down the steps, just about

walking on air back to my house. I didn't feel my broken toes, or even the shift of the coral shingle under my feet. I'd just had a beer with my Amazon of a next-door neighbour, I'd managed to keep from sticking my foot in my mouth for the duration and she'd not only agreed to give me a lot of money for a very simple job, she'd also invited me to dinner at her house.

I thought of the pilot who'd brought me here. He'd said these islands were cursed with murder, mutiny and lust. Well, he could take the first two and maybe the cursed, too. He was right about the lust, but it sure didn't seem like a curse to me.

My strangest house call story just got better. *The lady of the house threatened me with the rusty remains of a hammer, while I changed the fuel tank on her generator to save her ice cream, before she reimbursed me for my time with a beer and a dirty handshake. She offered me a repeat job with a huge paycheck. Then she asked me out.*

Nope, Dean still won't believe me.

BELINDA

Vanessa was waiting for us, her fingers curled around a cup, when we climbed aboard, fish in hand. *"The generator required repairing last night."*

"My apologies. As soon as I am dressed, I will..." Maria began.

Vanessa cut her off. *"It is already done."*

"Then you are becoming more familiar with the generator. I'm surprised that you had so little trouble, but as the repairs were probably very simple..." Her words faded into silence as she took in Vanessa's thunderous expression.

Vanessa's words were almost as curt as human speech, despite her use of our language. *"They appeared to be, but I would not know. The young human fisherman came to my assistance and restored the generator to working order. We now owe him a favour.*"

I expressed my surprise. "*You mean the young male human with the nice...*"

I thought of the mango in our freezer. I almost removed it to tell Vanessa why we had purchased the fruit, but I was stopped dead by her tone. "*You will not do anything to antagonise the young fisherman. You will not speak to him or go near him, unless it is absolutely necessary. And you will do no further repairs of the house or any part of the land camp. For this I will engage the human fisherman's services. Now we have lobsters to pull up.*"

Maria and I quickly retreated to the inside of the vessel and dressed. Vanessa followed us into the cabin, in search of something with which to restrain her hair. I offered her the pink ribbon she had rejected on sight when I had first shown it to her. She hesitated, then chose the blue elastic circles.

As I headed up the stairs, I glanced back and saw her examining the pink ribbon again. She began cutting it into short lengths with some scissors, before stuffing them into her pockets. I turned and continued up to the deck.

Maria and I hastened to untie the vessel and be under way. I wondered what kind of favour the young human fisherman would ask of her, and how much trouble it would be to provide it.

JOE

I watched Vanessa load up her crays on the carrier boat. Hers were bigger and fatter than ours, or, in fact, any of the other crates of lobsters.

"Are those the same lobsters as ours?" I asked her, lifting up a crate of ordinary-sized ones.

"Sort of," she said. "Mine are what yours would grow up to be, if you left them in the water another 20 years."

"Seriously?"

"Yes, these guys live up to 30 years. I just have a knack for catching the old-timers." She winked and lifted another crate of the monsters. They made ours look undersized, though I knew every one of ours wasn't. I'd measured the bastards myself.

I figured she wouldn't tell me, but I asked anyway. "So, what's your secret?"

"Everyone asks that." She laughed and looked at me for a moment, as if she were sizing me up, before she spoke again. "I tie a pink ribbon to every pot. The old ones like pink."

I laughed. "You can't be serious."

She shrugged. "Here, you try it." She pulled a pink ribbon out of her pocket. "You tie that in a bow at the top of the pot and see what happens."

I took the ribbon and tucked it into my shorts pocket. "I bet it doesn't do anything."

"What will you bet me?" she asked mischievously.

I thought for a moment. I could think of a hundred things I wanted from her, but not much I could offer her. Dinner sounded good, if only I could cook something halfway decent. "A six-pack of beer," I said finally.

"Done," she replied instantly. "I bet you a

six-pack of beer that you get at least one old-timer in the pot you tie that ribbon to."

"And if there's none, or they're all normal sized?" I asked.

"Then I owe you beer." She laughed. "Make sure you have a spare six-pack in the fridge." She headed back to her camp.

"You make sure my beer's chilled, too," I called after her.

She just laughed and kept going.

BELINDA

"Checking the buoys at the surface to identify our pots is time-consuming. You will place these on all of my pots, for ease of recognition beneath the water." Vanessa placed a handful of strips of pink ribbon on the deck.

I took the fabric and examined it. I recognised the ribbon she'd been cutting up in the sleep cabin. *"A brighter colour or a more durable material might be more appropriate. This fabric will rapidly decay in the water."*

Her tone was commanding, brooking no argument. *"You may examine other materials when you are next on the mainland. Now you will place the ribbons on the pots, until they decay beyond use. Then you will know which to fill with the old lobsters, without needing to look closely.*"

I looked askance after her as she marched down the jetty to her house. I turned to Maria. "*Does this seem peculiar to you?*"

"*It does. I suspect the troublesome young human fisherman is involved somehow,*" she replied.

I nodded. "*As do I.*"

JOE

"It's not good weather for them tomorrow. We'll only put down half as many, closer in. No point in putting them all out in bad weather," Skipper grumbled.

I admit the wind was picking up and the waves were stronger, but I didn't see how that affected the lobsters. I shrugged, not really fussed. *Only half the pots means only half the work tomorrow morning.*

I stuck my hands in my pockets to warm them up a bit. My fingers closed around Vanessa's pink ribbon.

"Hey, do you know why Vanessa gets bigger crays than anyone else?" I asked him.

"Nope. Her mother did that, too, and neither of them ever told me why." He shrugged. "Those are her pots over there, not far from ours. You'd think we'd get some big ones, too, but no one ever does, when they put their pots out near hers."

I held out the pink ribbon. "Vanessa told me she ties pink bows on her pots and the big ones are attracted to them."

He looked like he was considering his words carefully. "And you believe that?" he asked slowly.

He's wondering if I'm an absolute idiot, possibly even more stupid than his last deckie.

I laughed and he joined in. "No, actually. But I bet her some beer I'd try it and prove her wrong."

He stopped laughing. "Well, if there's beer at stake, maybe we should put another pot down. All prettied up with Vanessa's ribbon."

I tied the ribbon on myself and pushed the pot over the side.

BELINDA

"I swear she has put down more of these wooden boxes than usual. I have counted twice and both times the total is 61," Maria complained.

I shrugged as I responded. *"They all have ribbons on them. What is one more? Here, I have several lobsters which will not fit in my box. Place them in the last one and our task is complete."* I urged the lobsters toward her.

She pushed them into the box as the complaints continued. *"Why does she not fish like the humans, placing fish scraps in the box and leaving it to attract the spiny lobsters without assistance?"*

I repeated the answer Vanessa had given to us when I had asked her this question. *"Because she has ordered that we will only give the humans the lobsters that are near the end of their lives. That means singing the old ones from the depths and placing them in the boxes."*

"And if she does not obtain the information we seek before our fishing is complete?" Maria's expression was worried.

I kept my tone light. *"Then we will perhaps have some quiet nights, as she will decline to fish in order to extend our time here."*

Her expression darkened. *"Do you think it likely that our exile here will be extended?"*

Like my sister, I sincerely hoped not, but I said instead, *"She may need to do so, if her gathering of information does not progress."*

Maria's question took me by surprise. *"What do you think slows her progress?"*

I was thoughtful, so my reply was slow. *"Either the humans here have no further information to give, or she feels some attraction for the young human fisherman. She spends time in his company and avoids the task at hand."*

Maria voiced a possibility I had not considered. *"Is it possible that he holds information that the others do not? He is not a very experienced fisherman. From what I understand, his knowledge of fish or fishing is far less than most."*

I did not discount her idea, though I doubted it. *"Perhaps."*

Maria sounded suspicious. *"Or have we underestimated her preference for his shapely behind?"*

Even the thought of Vanessa with a preference for a human was ludicrous. I could not stop my laughter. When I did reply, it was in a more serious vein. *"Would you question her on her motives? I would not. She will reveal her purpose when she chooses and not before."* I changed the subject to lift her spirits. *"Come, our fishing is complete for a few hours. Shall we call up some dolphins and play?"*

Maria started to smile. *"Certainly. At least our exile here has its compensations, shallow water and dolphins to call."*

"Then let us make the most of it!" I started off with a flip of my tail.

JOE

As we pulled up the pots the following morning, Skipper kept grumbling. The catch was poor, the weather was bad, we should go in instead of wasting our time...

The last one we pulled up was full. I opened up the pot to let them out and gasped as the first one hit the bottom of the box. It was huge. So were the rest that fell in on top of it. My heart sinking, I looked at the top of the pot and there was Vanessa's pink ribbon, still tied in a bow.

Skipper looked at the catch and cracked a smile for the first time that morning. "Well, I guess it was worth going out today."

I pointed at the ribbon.

He laughed. "Now you owe Vanessa some beer. I told you to stay away from her!"

He started picking through the lobsters. They all looked like the monsters Vanessa had loaded onto the carrier boat earlier in the week. "I'll tell you what, though. As a deckie this lucky, I'll buy you a couple of beers in the Club tonight."

"Fair enough." I nodded.

We baited the pot up again and pushed it off the side, the ribbon still in place.

BELINDA

"*The human fishermen are aware of changes, but only as it affects their fishing. Their knowledge is limited. They discuss this among themselves as they cautiously describe their catch,*" I told Vanessa.

It was clear from her expression that I told her nothing new. "*I find the same and I have spoken to many. The Fisheries Officers appear more knowledgeable, but they defer to other humans for more information. I believe there may be more, but in order to find this out it will be necessary to communicate with the humans they refer to. Some other Fisheries office, in Perth? We may need to go further afield, unless the humans are to visit here. I will see who I can contact, to discover what I can. If we must go to Perth, then at the*" *end of the fishing season, we shall."*

My heart sank as a knocking at the door echoed loudly through the house. We shifted to a room with a window, where we could see the young human stood outside, his face all shiny.

I spoke first. *"It is the young fisherman. I believe he carries some beer."*

Vanessa's voice was quick, quiet and urgent. *"You will not speak to him, nor will you alert him to your presence. You will remain in my bedroom until he has left."*

I retreated to her bedroom. She glared at me until I shut the door. Then I heard her open the door which the human knocked at with such fervour.

I spoke the words aloud, though only she would hear and understand them. *"This young human fisherman is trouble. We do not hide from our sisters. Who is this human that I must hide from him?"*

JOE

After we got back, I showered and got changed into some clean clothes. I even shaved carefully. When I was as presentable as I could manage, I got a six-pack of Stella out of the fridge and headed over to Vanessa's place.

The *Siren* was tied up at the jetty and there was a fresh set of washing out on her veranda. I dodged through the washing to get to her front door.

I had to knock twice before she answered. She looked surprised to see me.

"What is it?" she asked, a piece of toast in her hand.

I held out the six-pack of beer. "You were right. The big lobsters like pink ribbons. I tried it on one of Skipper's pots last night and now he thinks I'm the luckiest deckie in the Abrolhos, if not the world. So, now I owe you some beer."

She put the toast down and took the beers. She looked as if she was puzzled by them. "But I can't drink all these by myself," she said. "Come over tonight and share them with me."

My heart soared and then sank, like a rotten lobster thrown over the side. "Skipper said we had to go to the club on Little Rat tonight. He wanted to buy me a beer."

Her face fell. "Well, when you can. Afterwards, maybe, or another night."

"I'll get out of the club as early as possible and come over tonight, if I can," I promised her eagerly. "Otherwise, tomorrow for sure."

She smiled. "I'd like that."

BELINDA

I told Maria of the conversation when I joined her in the water.

She enjoys the company of a human male? I do not understand. Who else among our people has dallied long enough with them to conceive more than one child? Except under necessary circumstances.

I looked at her in surprise. *"It's because of your father."*

Maria's confusion was palpable. *"But she spent only a few days and nights here and the deed was done. Then she swam home with me inside her. She did not linger."*

I was careful in my response, for it was difficult to believe she did not know. *"Did you never ask why Mother was absent when you were little?"*

Maria was bitter. *"Duty, the elders told me. She allowed it because she does not like me. I am a painful reminder of when duty required her to permit one of those dirty human males inside her."*

My voice was gentle. *"No. She spent only a brief time with your father, then swam home and announced to the elders that she would not do her duty."*

Maria let out a very human snort with a stream of bubbles. *"That would have gone down well. How could she say that when she already carried me?"*

I spoke as a healer, to one who knew little of such things. *"It was too early to tell. She did not know and nor did the elders. So when she defied them, she was instructed to do her duty, and not return until she had."*

"But she gave birth to me in the Nursery Grounds. She did not depart immediately." Maria's confusion lingered.

I explained the story Grandmother Sephira had told me, many years ago. *"No, she was permitted time to rest in the deep before she was* required to depart, and in that time she discovered she carried you. The elders permitted her to stay until you were weaned, but for her defiance the judgement still stood.

"She chose a rock island, far to the north of where she met your father. She hid in the caves beneath the island and roared her defiance at the cave walls, avoiding both her people and her duty. Yet the humans on the island heard her and one day one of them glimpsed her, swimming in the water. They called her a water dragon, for that was what she appeared to be to them.

"The island had a young, male human leader, who visited the caves with the other humans, to hear and see the dragon. She flipped her tail, angry, and dove deeper into the darkness of the water. She roared at them in the dark as she hid from them.

"The human leader returned to the cave often, alone. At first, he sat silent, watching for the dragon, and she remained silent and hidden. After a time, he started to speak to the dragon, as if she would speak to him, of trouble on the island and the difficulties he faced.

"She practised his language in the dark, until she could make the same sounds. One day he visited the cave, saddened by the damage a storm had wreaked on *the human settlement. She chose to appear human in a pool of water in the cave, to offer him comfort.*

"The human was surprised to see a human woman he did not know in that place. He asked her if she was the dragon, shifting form to look like a human woman.

"She had listened to many humans on the island. Could not human women, the wives of men on the island, turn into dragons? she asked him. Could she not be a human woman who chose to be a dragon more than she was a woman?

"He found her idea amusing and accepted her offer of comfort. He visited her often for this.

"She remained at the cave far too long, even after the human had stopped visiting her. Her time came early, whilst she remained in the island caves. Our kind heard her cries and helped her, in the dark beneath the island. They carried her and me to the deeps when she was strong enough. She named me for a water dragon."

Maria was shocked. *"How do you know all of this? You were far too young to remember, for some of it was before you were born."*

I told her the truth, for our people do not lie to one another. *"Grandmother told me, for she was one of the elders even then. Mother told this story to them on her return."*

Maria's next words revealed her limited contact with humans. *"Yet it does not explain why she might enjoy the company of another human now. After being required to do her duty twice, I expect her to feel revulsion for the human males."*

I tried to help her to understand. *"She became friends with the human male. I believe this shared liking makes the joining experience quite pleasurable. After all, she continued to engage in it with him long after she was aware she carried me."*

I did not succeed. Maria's expression was horrified. *"Even the thought disgusts me. "*

I tried to be conciliatory. Life on land had not been her calling. *"It is fortunate, then, that you could do your duty using the human technology they call artificial insemination."*

She gave another snort. *"It is fortunate for us all. It makes the duty bearable. Was Zerafina not also the result of this technology?"*

Bubbles of laughter, drifting up to the surface. I tried to control myself sufficiently to reply. *"Zerafina was the result of large quantities of alcoholic drink that burned my throat and time spent with a warm human male whose hair was the colour of fire."*

Her silence allowed me the luxury of remembering the experience. Of course I had named my daughter in memory of the nights of burning, alcohol-fuelled passion that created her.

Maria's words broke through my thoughts. *"I still do not understand the attraction."*

I made my voice soothing. *"Nor would I expect you to, Maria."*

Her attention was distracted by a small vessel on the surface. *"Oh, look, it's a fisherman, alone in a little metal boat. Do you think the human would be more attractive if he were to wash more frequently? Even a cold salt water wash would improve him."*

Wave, current, water, wind, depth, rock, push...

I could feel the wave build as she shaped it. In her anger, she put too much power in it, but it was too late to stop the wave before it crashed over the little metal boat.

"Now you've done it – his boat's a bathtub and it will sink unless we get it out of the water. Come on, let's put it up somewhere out of the water where he'll be safe."

Under the little metal boat, shaping the

waves to speed us in the right direction, we took it to a barely submerged rock and wedged the craft in.

"Now, let's leave this shag on his rock to dry out till morning." I led Maria back to the *Siren*.

JOE

"To the lucky deckie!" Skipper roared. All the beer glasses went up with a ragged cheer, before tipping to empty their contents down the throats of their owners.

My glass came down empty. I wiped my mouth with the back of my hand and stood up. I started to weave through people to the sink out the back. It was near closing time and there was an unspoken rule – it was always the deckies' turn to wash up.

Skipper stood in front of me, so I had to stop. "Not your turn tonight. You head back to camp." He winked. "Maybe find some other way to celebrate tonight."

Bloody bastard was reading my mind. I faked a yawn. "Yeah, like sleep before you get me up at the crack of dawn tomorrow." I stumbled out of the club into the dark.

Someone made a ribald comment behind me that I didn't hear, but the laughter in response was unmistakeable.

It took me a minute to find my torch in my pocket and switch it on, before I went down the rock-strewn track to the dinghy.

I pushed it out into the water and got in. The engine caught on the second pull and I steered her around, headed back to Rat Island and camp. Good thing I knew this stretch of water so well – beer and driving a boat in the pitch black was bloody difficult.

I figured I had maybe half an hour before the other guys would be back. If we had the lights out by then, maybe they wouldn't bother us. *Was that enough time for a couple of drinks with her? A drink or two and one thing might lead to another....SHIT!*

I felt the wave drench me from behind and saw it half fill the boat with water, knocking the torch out of my hand. The engine sputtered and died, drowned, and I found a few more four-letter words to describe the motor. I pulled on it, over and over, pounded it till my hand hurt, but the bitch didn't catch. Dead in the water, with a boat full of water, I groped for the paddle I know had been there before the wave hit. My hand grasped the handle and I pulled it free.

Look at the bloody lucky deckie now, I fumed. *Paddling his bloody dinghy back to Rat Island in the dark.*

I paddled till my arms ached, but the distant lights on Rat only seemed to get further away. I saw the other guys get in their dinghies and head back to Rat Island in a convoy. I shouted and waved, but they never heard me. The wind was blowing the wrong way, carrying my voice out to sea. It had picked up a fair bit, too.

I stopped paddling to rest for a few minutes, letting the boat drift with the waves. *Maybe it'll ground on a sandbank or a rock and I can just sit here and wait till morning.*

I hadn't prayed about it, but the unsaid prayer was answered anyway. The bottom of the boat scraped across a rock. I tipped the useless motor up, in an effort to save it from further damage, as the tinnie wedged up against part of the rock just under the surface. I breathed a sigh of relief.

Now I just sit here and have wet dreams while I'm soaked through in a dinghy full of water on a rock, until someone comes looking for me in daylight. Just the thought of Vanessa with her clothes off would keep any red-blooded male warm for a night...

I drifted between sleep and daydreams, waking every time a wave jolted the boat. Another wave sloshed over the side of the boat, soaking me again, and forcing me awake. The boat was almost full of water now, I realised in panic, as I groped for a bucket to start bailing with. Throwing bucket after bucket overboard, I couldn't tell if I was making any difference to the water level in the boat.

One moment I was holding the bucket, about to scoop up more water, the next I was flying through the air, full of spray and water and no sign of the tinny. Suddenly immersed in cold black water, I couldn't see the surface. I struggled, kicking in the direction I thought was up, and hit a rock. I jerked back reflexively and my head cleared the water. I gulped a huge lungful of air and grabbed for the rock. I had to hold on till daylight. Surely, that couldn't be too far away.

Another big wave and I tried to keep a hold of the slimy rock, but I was pushed out of reach, drifting in the current. I tried to kick my legs, but I wasn't sure if I did. I couldn't feel my feet and the numbness was creeping up my legs. *Vanessa won't be able to help me here*, I thought. I could feel my body shake with laughter. I drifted.

I could hear the breakers on the outer reef, louder than they were from shore. I could feel the spray on my face. A wave washed over me and I was under the water again.

I thought I heard dolphins, but it sounded deeper and closer with my head submerged. Dolphins or whales? I thought I could feel them beside me, rolling me over so my face was at the surface, pulling my body through the water.

Arms lifted me into a boat, laying me down across the length of it. *Dolphins with arms? No, that's not right.*

I could feel the boat moving through the water, but I couldn't hear the engine. Maybe it was the rushing in my ears, drowning it out. All I could hear was an unearthly singing, high and sad, like some kind of suicidal dolphin. I could say I blacked out, but everything was already so fucking black I wouldn't have noticed the difference.

I checked out of Hotel Consciousness. At least I got to dream of Vanessa naked.

BELINDA

Humans returning. Hidden from sight under a jetty, we watched them pass.

I lifted my head from the water to hear the conversation.

Vanessa walked out to meet them. "Where's Joe?" she asked. "Did he stay back to close up?"

A raucous laugh from one of them. "He came back early. He's probably asleep in his bunk, dreaming about you."

She laughed, but it sounded forced. She was worried.

She waited until they had returned to their camps before she came to us. We could not hide from her.

"*His little boat has not returned. He may need help. We must find him. I will bring my little boat. You help me. Have you seen him?*"

Maria answered, "*His little boat is stuck on a rock between the islands. It contains some water, but he will be safe until someone rescues him.*"

Vanessa proceeded from worry to incredulity. "*You saw him and left him in such a precarious position?*"

I defended my own role in the mess. "*Maria damaged his boat motor with a poorly placed wave. We felt it would be safest to place the boat there than let it drift without power.*"

Now Vanessa became angry. "*The young human fisherman has offered to fit out our land home with communications like that of the mainland. If we lose him, we must spend additional months on the mainland, away from our people. You will accompany me and you will find him. We must help him, whatever it takes. If you do not find him, on our return I will inform the elders that the delay was caused by your carelessness.*"

Her fury was palpable. She jumped into the small metal boat and started the motor. She moved the boat into the deeper water and headed for the gap between the islands, then to the open water between the island and the outer reef, searching.

We found his little metal boat, upside-down just below the surface. We tipped the water out and pushed it the right way up. She brought her boat over to us and tied a rope to his little vessel, towing it behind hers.

Her voice was anxious. *"Find him. He must be close."*

Near the barrier reef, I saw him.

I called for my sister. *"Maria. Quickly, he is by the outer reef. He cannot swim, so we must take him together."*

Maria and I carefully lifted the human to the surface. Vanessa looked relieved, but her voice was still anxious. *"Bring him to the boat."*

She leaped from her boat to his, her aim so perfect that both vessels barely rocked. She dropped to her knees and held out her arms. We helped her to lift him into the boat. She didn't let go of him, even when he was securely out of the water.

I watched her for a moment, as she held

tight to the cold, wet human, her expression worried. I relented and gave her advice, as a healer who had been trained in human health as well as that of our own people. *"He is colder than a human should be. He needs warmth."*

Her eyes were cold. *"Then we must make him dry and warm."*

Looking at the human she held in her arms, his head resting on her breasts, I voiced both Maria's and my wish. *"I feel you are all the warmth he wishes for."*

Vanessa's anger had softened in her concern for the human, but it was not gone. *"After the trouble both of you have caused, it should be you girls who assist him to recover. However, as it appears I can trust neither of you with his well-being, this will be my responsibility. I will find another way for you to make amends. For now, Belinda will steer my boat, whilst Maria will guide us."*

Together, we guided both metal vessels back to the jetty through the waves, as she raised her voice to sing him to sleep. Her song was powerful and his sleep was deep.

We assisted her to transfer the human from the boat to a wheelbarrow on the jetty. She took him back to his dwelling alone.

We took his boat back to its usual floating place, tying it up securely.

We retired for the night, but she remained to care for the human. She devoted considerable time and effort to ensuring his well-being, leaving his house not long before dawn. She returned to her own house for long enough to wash and change her clothes. She then returned to the jetty.

I politely enquired after the human's health. *"Is the human warm enough for your liking?"*

"Oh yes. He is very warm." Vanessa smiled. Her hands rubbed her upper arms slowly. She turned away to step into the boat cabin. Both Maria and I breathed a sigh of relief that we were not required to further tend to the human.

"Time to go and pull the pots." Vanessa's eyes were bright and excited.

I wondered what could be so exciting about lobsters, today as opposed to any other day.

JOE

I dreamed of Vanessa. Tonight the dreams were more explicit than ever. She came to me in a blue lace g-string and woke me up with a stellar blow job. Then we had sex in every position I'd ever heard of and a couple I swear I imagined. A hell of a dream.

What woke me from it was the sound of a boat engine. *You went to sleep on a rock. You need to wake up to get their attention and get rescued.*

Reluctantly, I opened my eyes. It was dark, but it felt like I was in bed, not out on the reef. I felt around. Blankets, sheets, mattress – not usually stuff found on a reef. I sat up. Hmm, I was buck naked, too. Also not something I was stupid enough to be out on the reef.

I got up. *Yep, I dreamed of Vanessa last night. Now the sheets need a wash.*

I pulled the sheets off the bed and bundled them into my arms, padding across to the laundry on the other side of the shack. There was a load already in the washing machine, clothes clinging to the outside of the drum as if they'd finished a full cycle. I pulled the wet stuff out, dumping it in the tub that I used as a laundry basket. *Huh. Those are the clothes I wore yesterday. Don't remember putting a load of washing on. Fuck, I don't remember getting home.*

I shoved the sheets in the machine and turned it on. Then I hunted up a pair of shorts and put them on, before going outside in the pre-dawn light to hang out the damp washing on the clothesline next to my donga.

Skipper was walking down the track, almost at the jetty, with another skipper I didn't recognise in the poor light. "Morning."

I nodded in reply and followed him down the jetty. The tinny was there, tied up where I always left it. The paddle was lying in the bottom of the boat, across some big dents that hadn't been there yesterday. I knelt on the jetty and pulled at the rope. I hadn't tied those knots, I was sure of it.

Behind me, Skipper laughed and I jumped. "Looks like you banged the dinghy up pretty good last night. Sounds like it was the only banging you got up to, though – Vanessa was looking for you last night, but you'd already gone to bed."

Vanessa. I looked over at her jetty, but her boat was already gone. Like every other morning, out of the anchorage before I was even up. Good thing, too, this morning – I'd have trouble looking at her without thinking of that damn blue g-string. *An imaginary blue g-string,* I reminded myself.

"Ready to go?" Skipper asked.

I shook my head, trying to shake out the graphic pictures rattling around inside it. "Lemme grab a shirt."

I went inside and grabbed the first shirt I found. I pulled it on over my head as I wandered down the jetty to the fishing boat.

"Time to go pull the pots and count the crays."

I got to work, untying the ropes from the jetty, my arms aching in memory of my paddling attempts last night. When I had all the ropes back aboard the boat, Skipper started to pull away from the jetty into the anchorage channel, heading south, as the sun crept over the horizon.

As we passed her house, I saw her washing hanging out on her veranda, too. I realised that the g-string wasn't imaginary, because there it was, moving in the breeze. I must have seen it on the washing line before and forgotten, though not completely. I looked more closely at the line of small lace items, which would be hidden from view from the path by the row of shirts and shorts, unless the wind blew the shirts up out of the way, like they just did. That wasn't what held my attention, though. *All of her underwear is blue. Hell, all of her clothes are some shade of blue, from her jacket to the tiny lace g-string.*

Fuck, what I'd give to see her in it. This daydream lasted until we were well out of the anchorage channel.

"Hey, it looks like someone's lost a torch." Skipper pointed at the rocks at the southern end of the island's western beach, bringing my attention back to the present reality.

I glanced at it, not needing more than a glance to know it was mine. *I'll walk over and pick it up after work*, I told myself.

"Everything that's lost on the reefs washes up here. Even found a dead body here once," Skipper said.

A dead body. The chill from this was more effective than any cold shower. "Who?"

"Oh, it was more'n fifty years ago. Some bloke who got washed overboard in a cyclone. His body washed up here a couple of weeks later. They buried him up on the cliff." He pointed at the white cross on top of the cliff that I'd never noticed before.

The chill went bone-deep. *That's where I would have ended up last night, if I hadn't made it home. Now, how did I make it home?*

BELINDA

"Why is one human so important to her? She could get another human to install her technology." Maria's grumbling resonated with my uneasy thoughts.

"She tries to make amends for losing your father. Has she not told you this?"

Her response came unwillingly. *"He was a human fisherman. She does not speak of him to me."*

Again, I found myself repeating a tale Grandmother Sephira had told me. *"She came to these islands in a big storm. A storm so powerful the waves washed over the land and claimed it once more. She was swimming in the strong waves, when she saw a little fishing boat overturned. Two men were struggling in the water. One swam with a rope, but he lost it. The other could not swim and the waves pushed him under to where she drifted. She gave him air and took him to shore. She tended to his hurts and shared her warmth with him until the storm died down…"*

Maria interrupted with impatience, *"And I am the result. A storm child, indeed. What has this to do with the human fisherman today?"*

Undeterred, I continued, *"After he had rested, she swam him back to his people. His wounds bled and called the sharks. She sent the sharks away, but lost him in the water. When she found him, no air she gave him could bring him back. Death had claimed him."*

"But that was long ago. More than ninety years. How can the loss of one human so long ago matter to anyone now?" She sounded puzzled.

I attempted to explain. *"It matters to her. His memory haunts her still, as she mourns his loss."*

Her disbelief was clear in her expression. *"Surely not."*

I lifted my head above the surface and waited for her to do the same. *"Of course it does. He called her Maria, thinking her an angel. She gifted this name to you, forever a reminder of her time with this man. It is far better than the name she chose for me. At least she did not call you a dragon! See for yourself. She stands on the cliff where his body was buried, shedding salt water for his memory."*

We both watched Vanessa stand on the cliff, her tears glistening in the starlight.

"Are you so sure she does not cry in memory of the pain he caused her, when he used her body?"

I suppressed my amazement that she knew our mother so little. I replied as calmly as I could, *"I am certain, for she presses her lips to the stone that marks his head and the words she whispers express sorrow and her desire for his forgiveness. If he had caused her pain that saddened her now, she would not hesitate to give his remains to the ocean. She would feed his bones and the stone bearing his name to the sharks. While she desires forgiveness, she does not forgive."*

Maria reflected before responding. *"Perhaps you are correct. It seems difficult to believe, even so."*

I reminded myself that Maria had never known the touch of a man. I tried to be patient. *"As you said before, you do not understand the attraction. Presumably, you would not also understand her feeling of loss when the object of the attraction is gone."*

I hid both my smile and my satisfaction as

she confirmed my surmise.

"*Undoubtedly. I think I do not understand her at all.*"

JOE

When we returned to the anchorage, the *Siren* was tied up at her jetty again.

I helped Skipper with the gear and the catch before I dragged myself back to my shack. Dead tired, I just wanted to climb back into bed and go to sleep, but I owed Vanessa an apology for standing her up last night.

I knocked on her door, but I got no answer. I walked up the jetty to the *Siren* and called her name, but there was no answer there, either, from Vanessa or her deckies.

Finally, I gave up and went home to bed. I was gone as soon as my head touched the pillow.

It was mid-afternoon when I woke up. I tried Vanessa's house again, but still she wasn't home.

I made a sandwich from some of the food in the fridge and headed across the island to retrieve my torch. It sported a few dents and there was water inside it, but I figured if I took it back to my shack and dried it out, it might still work. I could put it on the veranda, next to my lobster-scented steel-capped boots.

I could see the gravestone we'd spotted from the water this morning and I went further up the path to take a look.

The marble cross was chipped, so some of the words were missing, but the name and date were still clear enough.

His name was Giuseppe and he died in 1921, more than 90 years ago. I felt the chill, again. *Giuseppe, just like me. I bet they never called him Joe.*

I looked to the south, toward Little Rat Island. I could see the beach where I'd anchored the dinghy. It seemed such a short distance away, but last night it had seemed like the channel between the islands stretched forever. I turned my back on it and walked north, alongside the airstrip.

There was a little beach here that I'd seen from the air and the water, but this was the first time I'd walked along it. A sleepy seal was sprawled across my path, so I turned around and went back up to the track. I sat on the cliff, facing the outer reefs that had been so close in the dark last night, but were out of sight from the island. The sun was sinking. It wasn't far above the waves now.

Not wanting to go back yet, I just sat there and watched the waves rolling, the sun setting and the stars appearing, as I let my mind drift. The stars spread across the sky, a Milky Way you never saw in Perth; only in the middle of nowhere – inland or out here. If it weren't for the constant wind, the sound of the waves and surf, the peeping birds and the distant noise of generators, I could almost be back at any of our remote camps. *No, there's no snoring. It's not an outback camp unless some bastard's snoring.*

I could feel myself smiling in the dark. I clambered to my feet, turning toward the camps to head back. I could see the faint lights in the distance, but between them and me was a sea of blackness, full of treacherous rocks waiting to trip me up. *Shit. I should have brought a torch.* I remembered the metal cylinder I clutched in my hand and tried to switch it on. *No, it's still too wet to work. I should have brought a torch that works.*

I stumbled away from the cliff, hoping I'd hear when my footsteps reached the gravel airstrip. My feet were still on sand when I bumped into someone.

"Oh, sorry!" Vanessa's voice sounded as shocked as I felt.

"Vanessa?" I asked.

"Yes. What are you doing out here, Joe? Did you come looking for me?" Her voice sounded watery, as if she'd been crying.

For the life of me, I didn't have the guts to ask what had upset her. "I came looking for you earlier. I knocked on your door a few times, but you weren't home, so I went for a walk. I dropped my torch in the water and it's stopped working, so now I'm kind of stuck stumbling home in the dark." A sudden thought struck me. *What if she was upset because I hadn't turned up last night?* "I wanted to apologise for last night. I got back so late I don't remember how I got home. I don't even remember getting into bed."

"No worries," she said softly. "Would you like to have a drink with me tonight instead?"

"Sure," I replied without thinking. After a moment, I added, "If we can manage to get back to your camp in the pitch dark."

She laughed. "I think my eyesight might be better than yours, or maybe it's just my night vision. Let me help you home."

Her cool fingers crept around my arm and she moved closer to my side, so close I could feel the heat of her. I thought I was imagining it, until my thigh brushed against hers and I realised she really was that close to me.

She didn't say anything or move away, so I didn't voice the apology on the tip of my tongue.

When our feet crunched on the gravel of the airstrip, noisier by far than the whisper of sand, I breathed a sigh of relief. She laughed at me.

"Why, don't you trust me?" she teased.

"It's just that it's so dark," I explained. "I don't know how you can see anything."

She laughed again, but didn't say anything else. After a while, the crunching gravel gave way to the tinkling coral path, on the other side of the airstrip that led back to camp.

"You're good," I told her, impressed.

Another laugh in the dark. "I know."

There was more chance of stumbling now, with the shifting, uneven path, but her feet were sure and the few times I did stumble, her grip on my arm was enough to steady me so I didn't fall flat on my face. Vanessa guided me to her house, not letting go of my arm until she had to open the door. The golden light spilling out onto the deck was blinding after the darkness, so I stood on the veranda to let my eyes adjust.

"Come in," she called, already opening the fridge. "Have you had dinner?" she asked, as I stepped over the threshold.

"No," I admitted. "I should probably go home and grab something to eat before I drink too much."

Her face lit up. "I have some pork sausages

the girls brought over from Geraldton and the last of the field mushrooms. We could put them all on the barbeque."

Somehow I ended up standing at the barbeque on her veranda with a pair of tongs, turning the sausages whilst she did something in the kitchen with the mushrooms. When the smell from the sausages was making my stomach cramp in hunger, I called out to her, "I think the sausages are almost ready. Where do you want me to put them?"

Vanessa came out holding a dish of mushrooms, which she dumped on the barbeque. Then she handed me a plate for the sausages. "Only a minute each side for the mushrooms."

I loaded up the plate with the sausages, hoping I hadn't missed any, then piled the mushrooms on top. I carried it slowly into her kitchen, where she'd set the table. She'd even opened two beers.

She picked up one of the fat pork sausages in her fingers and bit it almost in half before I'd sat down. I stared at her, stunned, then looked away before she caught me staring.

*The thought of her putting that much of the long pink sausage into her mouth and then biting down...*I had a flashback from my vivid dreams of last night. I sat down hurriedly, pulling my chair right up to the table, and tried to concentrate on eating dinner.

Neither of us spoke much as we ate. I was terrified of saying something wrong and she seemed too dreamy and thoughtful to notice the lack of conversation. When we were both finished, she offered me another beer.

I was already sleepy from the one and I was worried I might inadvertently blurt out something I shouldn't if I drank anymore, so I declined, getting up to go home.

"You'll have to come over again to help me finish the rest of them," she said and I nodded.

I thanked her for the dinner and the beer, stumbling over my words, not sure if I was even coherent.

She seemed to understand and followed to see me out. As I stepped off her veranda, she asked me to wait.

I was shocked at the feel of her lips on my cheek. "Thank you," she said.

I stumbled down the path to my place. I remembered getting home this time and getting into bed. I lay awake for a while, thinking about Vanessa. After a while, my daydreams drifted into the night-time variety and I fell asleep.

BELINDA

After a night of swimming and fishing, followed by morning fishing with the vessel, Maria and I usually retired to the vessel's bunks to sleep until the sun sank from view. Today, I wished to sit on the deck a little longer, so Maria descended to the bunks without me.

The humans were awake, too. Fishing vessels were returning to their jetties. I saw more humans in the early afternoon than any other time of day. They tied up and unloaded their vessels, called out between jetties and the island and went into their houses.

The *Dolphin* cruised along the anchorage.

Skipper nodded and waved to me and I replied in kind. He did not smile, so I did not have to smile in response. The young human fisherman Vanessa liked so much stood on the deck of the *Dolphin*, but he did not see me as he watched the houses on the island. I suspected he looked for her, but she was not in sight. Like Maria, she slept.

I had not seen any of the other humans as entranced by her as this one was. It made him appear young and sweet, even though he was an adult human. I understood that she would enjoy his company. Last night, when her thoughts were saddened by a human long since dead, he brought a smile to her lips.

She worked hard for our people and she sought to help the humans, too. It hurt her when her efforts failed, but they did not diminish. She was perpetually worried for the future of our people and of the humans. If she could save us all, she would. If she could not, she would teach us to save ourselves.

I looked at the young human who was so mesmerised by her body. Would he be so eager for her if he knew that the last human man she had willingly touched was my father, more than 80 years in the past? At least this knowledge would crush his unrealistic hopes. Our kind do not willingly touch humans, except where duty requires it. She has borne two children for her people. She has no need to touch a human again.

I watched him assist Skipper in tying up the *Dolphin* and unloading their catch of the morning. Though not as practised in fishing as Skipper, the young human did not make mistakes. He was capable with his hands, carrying out his deckhand duties as Maria or I might. In six weeks, he had learned a considerable amount. I resolved to tell Vanessa this when she awoke. If she were required to return to land and fish with the *Siren* once more, she could employ him as a human deckhand, without the need for Maria or me.

As he stepped ashore from the vessel, he was addressed by a fisherman from one of the smaller islands. Roma Island, perhaps. He listened to the fisherman, looking concerned, then retrieved a heavy-looking bag from his veranda. Lifting the bag onto his shoulder, he followed the Roma fisherman to his vessel and was soon on his way south.

JOE

The story of Vanessa's generator and the Fisheries installation had spread across the island and then across the water. I went from being the newest deckie at the Abrolhos to the miracle sparky who could fix anything. I had skippers offering to do my deckie duties while I fixed their wiring. Skipper turned them down, refusing to take any other skipper over his "lucky deckie" on his boat, which meant my hours off the boat were suddenly in demand. I no longer had clean-up duties at the club.

It was almost two weeks later before I could keep my eyes open after dark. I seemed to step off the boat from the day's fishing only to be accosted by someone who needed an electrician to replace corroded wiring, repair the generator or take a look at their satellite dish. By the time I got home, with a pocket full of cash, an armload more beer and a stomach full of whatever dinner the happy fisher was only too pleased to share with me, I barely managed to collapse on my bed before I was out for the night.

On Friday night, I found myself home before dark, as a job that had looked really difficult turned out to be five minutes of reconnecting wiring. For the first time in a week, I was forced to rely on my own meagre cooking skills. As I finished up my dinner, I thought about what I might do that evening. I figured I'd manage to stay awake for a couple of hours yet. My first thought was to get out of my shack, so no one could bang on my door to ask me to come over and just take a look at their…whatever. The *whatever* would still need fixing tomorrow and I wanted a night off.

Once out of my place, my feet carried me to Vanessa's veranda, almost of their own volition. I knocked on the door. I heard her swear, before I heard her approach. She swung the door open.

I'd backed away from the door when I'd heard her swear. It was safer to be off the veranda and headed home if she didn't want me there.

"Who is it?" she asked, peering into the dark. She wore a pale blue singlet top with her little shorts today, giving me a tantalising view of her cleavage from clear across the veranda. In her hands was a bowl of ice cream. She lifted a spoon to her mouth, which hovered in mid-air when she noticed me.

She jumped in surprise. "Joe! What can I help you with?" The ice cream jumped with her – right off the spoon to splatter on her chest. It melted quickly on her warm skin, trickling between her breasts in a milky pink smear. She looked down. "Oh shit."

She swiped ineffectually at the ice cream with her hand, then snatched up a tea towel and dabbed at herself.

I want to bury my face in your boobs and taste that ice cream.

I realised I was staring at her and looked away, hoping she hadn't noticed.

"I'm sorry, Joe," she said. "Help yourself to a beer and some ice cream, if you like. I'll just go get cleaned up and put on a fresh shirt." She hurried out of the kitchen.

*Oh my God. What I'd give for you to take that singlet off and let me lick ice cream from your tits. You wouldn't even need a fresh shirt...*I bit my tongue so I wouldn't voice the offer I was dying to make.

I went over to the fridge and pulled out a beer.

"There. That's better," Vanessa said cheerfully behind me.

I turned around, taking a mouthful of beer. I almost spat it out again.

She'd evidently cleaned herself up in the bathroom and put on an equally pale blue t-shirt instead. She'd forgotten to dry herself, though, and I could see her blue lace bra clearly through the transparent t-shirt clinging to her damp skin.

"So did you want to go drink on the veranda or stay in here?" she asked me, getting herself a beer from the fridge.

"Oh, in here, I guess," I stammered. *The light's better in the kitchen and this is a view I do not want to miss*, I thought, as I sat across from her at the kitchen table.

That night I dreamed about Vanessa in blue lace.

BELINDA

"Some humans plan to speak to the fishers regarding changes to the oceans and changes to rules next week. They will fly here and speak of these matters in the Fisheries camp. We should attend, and take the time to question the human visitors closely. Perhaps we can avoid a trip to Perth." Vanessa's words took me by surprise. She had limited our contact with humans, after the incident with the deckhand.

Maria's surprise was no less than mine, but she spoke first. *"You wish us to attend? You understand the human terminology best, so you should be the one to question the humans."*

"If we all attend, we will recall more," Vanessa explained. *"However, I can ask all of our questions if*

you feel your human vocabulary is too limited. There are other changes to rules. The fishers I have spoken to suggest that fishing rules will change so that I must live on land in this camp more frequently than heretofore. I may have to fish one year in five, in order to retain our facilities here."

I spoke up. *"In that case, I recommend you look at engaging human crew. The young human fisherman we saved the other night is capable."*

Vanessa laughed. *"I would like to see how capable the man is, before I engage his services, or trust him with anything belonging to our people. This includes our properties on land and our vessel."*

"The humans believe he is very capable at maintaining human buildings. You, yourself, indicated you were impressed by his assistance in repairing the generator for your land camp," I replied defensively.

Vanessa smiled. *"But I do not know how he handles a vessel, nor how careful he is. If I must employ a human, I must be entirely satisfied that the human can be trusted."*

Maria was impatient. *"Enough of the human. Undoubtedly, you will have opportunities to observe his performance, before any such decision must be made. Is this not true?"*

Vanessa's smile grew more pronounced. *"It is. I will make sure such opportunities arise. So, we are agreed that we will all attend the human speeches at the Fisheries camp next week?"*

I answered her question, buoyed by the hope of soon seeing my daughter. *"Yes, we are agreed. Do you think the humans will give us enough information for us to return home next week, after the speeches?"*

Vanessa considered before she replied. *"Perhaps. I doubt it. I suspect further communication with the humans will be necessary. If we had better communication with the mainland, it might be possible to leave in two weeks. I will speak to Joe tomorrow regarding the communications technology. He ordered it some time ago and indicated it should arrive this week."*

I made a suggestion as it came to me. *"You can perhaps observe his performance in installing the communications technology."*

"I intend to observe his performance closely." Her tone held a meaning I could not fathom.

JOE

"Your gear's on the carrier boat. Come get it this afternoon," the note on my door read when we returned from fishing on the *Dolphin*. Instead of going in to make breakfast, I wandered down to the carrier boat jetty with a wheelbarrow I borrowed from Skipper.

"Hey, Joe," said Dave, the carrier boat skipper. "You got some electrical equipment here. Have the Fisheries boys broken their antenna again?"

I checked over the boxes, to make sure we had everything. "Nah, this isn't for Fisheries. I fixed their camp already."

"Who else wants a satellite link out here?"

Dave wondered.

I started lifting the boxes into the wheelbarrow. "Vanessa, *Siren*'s skipper. She said she wants internet access, and she's willing to pay for it."

Dave whistled. "Yeah, well if I looked like her, maybe I'd be able to afford a satellite link, too." He winked.

Annoyed, I snapped back, "She pays cash, like anyone else. I'm charging her the same as the Fisheries blokes." *If I give a discount to every client with a nice pair of boobs, I'll never get my house.*

He shrugged. "But I bet you'd give her a freebie for a night with her." His look turned shrewd. "I know I would."

My breath caught in my throat. *For a night with her, I'd probably be willing to pay for the equipment, too.* I shook my head and smiled. "Who wouldn't? But we'd never dare ask and we sure as hell wouldn't get it, even if we did ask. I'll take her money and be happy with that."

We both laughed. I finished loading up my wheelbarrow, thanked him and started carting the boxes away, down the path to Vanessa's place.

She was sitting on her veranda when I started unloading the contents of my wheelbarrow onto her deck. "Hi, Joe," she said, standing up and putting her book down. "Did you bring me a present?"

I laughed. "Just your communications equipment. It arrived on the carrier boat today. I can probably get it installed by tonight, if you like."

Her face lit up and she bounced with excitement. She was wearing one of those low-cut singlet tops again today. "Is there anything I can do?"

Look at those boobs bounce. Shit, I want to get my hands around those curves. No, don't stare at her boobs. Look up, damn it! "Well, if you want to make me that dinner tonight, I can work through till dark and get it finished today," I said carefully, praying that she didn't think I meant that all she could do was cook. She seemed quite liberated enough to hit me for suggesting she limit herself to cooking.

"Oooh, what do you want?" She was too excited to take offence, thank God.

You. "Whatever you like," I said vaguely, opening up boxes.

She headed back into the house. I went to get my tools and she was still inside when I got back. I got to work.

I was on her tin roof, setting up the satellite dish, when I heard her call my name. I stood up, looking around.

I saw her, almost underneath me, standing close to the eaves of her house. From this angle, I could see right down her singlet top to the pale blue lace inside it. *Oh, thank God I'm a sparky. Sights like this make it all worthwhile.*

"Did you want fish, steak, or pizza?" she asked, looking up at me. "The girls have some fresh fish, but I have some steak and frozen pizzas in the deep freeze."

"I haven't had a pizza in ages," I told her honestly.

She smiled. "Oh good, that's what I wanted, too, but I didn't want to be lazy and just heat up a frozen pizza when I promised you dinner. You're working so hard."

If I stretch out on the roof and stick my arms off the eaves, I can probably just reach those amazing tits, scoop them out of that lace…working hard, yeah.

I forced myself to turn my eyes back to the dish. *The satellite dish,* I reminded myself. After a few minutes, I dared to glance back to see if she'd gone back inside the house. She was still standing there, watching me.

"The pizzas only take twenty minutes, and I'm not hungry yet. Do you mind if I watch you?" she asked.

"Go ahead," I told her. *Just as long as you don't mind me watching you…right, get this satellite dish fixed to the roof, then you can take another look. Only a few seconds, or she'll notice you staring. Then you have to get it wired up before you get another one…God I love being a sparky.*

I did everything I possibly could from the roof before I reluctantly climbed down. I drilled a few holes, wired it all up, installed the equipment inside the house…it went faster than the Fisheries camp, because her house was much smaller and it was a completely new installation. The sun was setting as I finished and her house smelled pretty strongly of pizza.

I checked the signal and it was surprisingly good. "I'll hook up your phone, if you like," I offered.

She laughed. "Um, I haven't bought one yet. I'll get the girls to pick one up next time they go to the mainland. It's the internet I really want, for my laptop." She pointed at the black bag that blended in to the rickety little black table pushed up against the wall behind the fridge.

I unzipped the bag and starting setting up her laptop, plugging it in to power and the uplink, before turning it on. As the little computer started up, I debated in my head what her desktop picture would be. *Kittens. Puppies. Some girly movie. Please, don't let it be some stupid buff actor. Please, don't let it be a bloke at all. Horses. Fish. Dolphins…yeah, I bet she has a pretty picture of dolphins.* I waited and was disappointed to see the ordinary, default blue background. *I would have picked Vanessa for someone who'd choose her own.*

A window popped up, asking me for a password. I drew a blank. "Vanessa? It's asking for your password."

I could hear her footsteps on the vinyl. Two arms came around my neck, fingers reaching for the keyboard. She rested her chin on my shoulder, her boobs squashed against my back. I sat frozen for a second, until I realised that she couldn't quite touch the keyboard.

"Did you want me to move?" I asked breathlessly.

"No," she said vaguely. She moved back, so she wasn't touching me anymore. I dared to breathe again.

She touched her fingers to my shoulder, walking around to stand next to me. As naturally as if this were a perfectly normal thing to do, she perched on my lap.

I didn't know where to put my hands or what to say. I pressed my legs together and desperately prayed I didn't get too turned on. Most of me wanted her to sit there long enough for me to get aroused, while a small part of me wanted her to get off the leg that was slowly going numb under her weight. *All of me wants her to redistribute her weight, put one leg on either side of me and get really close…*

She jumped up and I rubbed my leg as the returning circulation was painful. "Sorry, Joe," she said. "I'll get dinner."

While my mind wandered, she'd entered her password. I started checking her connections, until I heard the scrape of metal torturing metal in the kitchen. I looked up. Vanessa had a big knife and was trying to cut the pizza with it, sawing it down to the metal tray. She was putting a fair bit of effort into it, her boobs bouncing around in that singlet. If I watched her do this much longer, I was going to make a total idiot of myself and do something stupid.

I stood up and moved to the kitchen. "Let me help." I didn't know what I was doing, either, but I figured I should offer. *It beat watching and wishing.*

She put the knife down on the bench and stood back.

"What we need is one of those curved pizza knives, like a big saw, that the pizza shops have," I stated, trying to sound knowledgeable. "So, do you have one of those?"

She yanked open her kitchen drawer. I peered in and realised she'd picked the biggest knife she had. "Ah," I said uselessly.

"Do you have one in your place?" Vanessa asked brightly.

I have three knives. Two butter knives and one that looks sharper than the butter knives, but it isn't. Then there's the filleting knife in my fishing tacklebox...

I answered truthfully, "No."

We both stared at the pizza. *Well, if I were at home, I'd just pick up a knife and fork and cut it into bite sized pieces...*

"If we get a fork, maybe we can still cut it with the big knife," I suggested.

She pulled a fork out of the drawer and held it up with the knife. The look she gave me was trusting. "Now what?"

"Now you stab it with the fork and try to cut it..." I began.

She looked expectant. "Show me." But she didn't let go of her cutlery.

Cautiously, I put my hands over hers, grasping both of her hands, the knife and the fork. I took a deep breath and tried to help her cut the damn pizza into vague slices. I didn't let go of her hands till we'd finished. My hands felt like they were burning in contact with hers, but hers were cool as if this were perfectly normal. She dropped the knife and fork on the tray as soon as I let go of her hands.

"Thank you," she said, reaching for a mutilated slice of pizza. She took a big bite, before producing a plate to put the slice on. She chewed and swallowed. "Can I get you a drink?"

I was closer to the fridge. "I can get it. Did you want one, too?"

She nodded. "I'd like a beer, please."

I took out two beers, opened them and handed one to her. *These look like the Stellas I gave her.* I shrugged and drank it anyway. *Nothing wrong with a Stella.*

She sat at the kitchen table and I followed suit, figuring it would look bad if I went to sit on the couch. She waited while I took a huge bite of pizza and a big swig of beer before she spoke. "So, Mr Communications Expert, where'd you learn to hack up pizza like that?"

I almost choked. *Mr Communications Expert, who can barely manage a coherent sentence around her. I almost put the satellite dish the wrong way round, because I got distracted by her boobs.*

She leaned across the table, to pound me on the back. Her boobs almost spilled out the front of her singlet, right across the table. "Are you okay?" she asked anxiously.

I managed to swallow. Infinitely harder, I managed to drag my eyes away from her skin against the tabletop and look at her face. "Sure." I coughed. "Um, I don't know. Sometimes you just have to improvise with whatever's around."

"What's the dodgiest job you've ever had to do?" she asked.

Ripping you off for this installation, probably. I tried not to think about it. "Last week, one of the houses over on Roma had to be completely rewired, but I'd run out of spare wire and solder for the soldering iron, so I patched the whole thing up with a couple of rolls of electrical tape. And the fisher paid me well for it, too, because it meant his power worked. When the carrier boat got in with my supplies, I went back and fixed the whole place up properly. Then the fisher paid me all over again. I didn't have the heart to tell him that he'd been living in a house that was barely held together with sticky tape." We both laughed.

"Ooh, that reminds me," she said. I felt my heart sink. She pulled a folded wad of notes out of the hip pocket of her shorts and handed it to me. "That's how much you quoted me."

I took the cash, still warm from her body. My honesty got the better of me. "Look, I can't take all this. The Fisheries camp was a much harder job that took longer. Yours was easy by comparison…" I peeled off half the notes and tried to hand them back to her. I put the rest of the warm notes in my hip pocket. *This is the closest I'll ever be to getting into her pants.* "This is more than enough."

She folded my fingers around the notes I held out to her. "Keep it. I agreed to pay the quoted price because it's worth it to have internet out here." Her eyes turned wicked. "You could buy yourself a proper pizza knife and never have to eat hacked-up pizza again!"

It was my turn to laugh. "First I'd have to learn to use it. I'd still be eating a lot more hacked up pizza, till I work that out."

Her eyes shone. "What else do we have to do out here at night? We could share a few pizzas and you could work on improving your skills." *Was it my imagination, or did it seem like she wasn't talking about my talent for cutting pizza? Nah, must be just wishful thinking.*

Reluctantly, I put the extra money in my pocket and went to get some more pizza. We were both quiet for a bit, because even hacked up, the pizza was good.

When I didn't think I could eat any more, I started feeling guilty again for overcharging her. I stood up to leave, feeling bad that I was trespassing on her hospitality on top of ripping her off. I thanked her for the dinner as I walked toward her front door. I got the door open, before I turned back.

"If you ever need help with anything, just ask. I won't charge you a cent next time." I turned and walked out, closing the door behind me. I didn't even want to look at her.

You just ripped off a beautiful woman for letting you look at her boobs for half the day, while hooking up a few wires in her house. And all this so you can buy a house.

I lay face-down on my bed and stuck a pillow over my head. After a day of looking at her, I tried to shove Vanessa out of my mind and not think about her at all. I managed it until I fell asleep and lost all control of my thoughts entirely.

BELINDA

I entered Vanessa's house to wash the soiled clothing with her washing machine. She paid little attention to my presence, her eyes on the small computer screen. The coloured light from it shimmered like sunlight on shell.

I started a washing cycle for the clothing and returned to the kitchen, where Vanessa did not appear to have moved. I looked at her clam-like computer with distaste. *"You spend too much time with that machine. It has been more than a week and you have not left the house, not even to accompany us fishing. I have seen the young human fisherman knock at your door, only to receive no answer. Are you well?"*

Vanessa did not move and continued staring intently at the screen. I noticed two small wires running from the side of the computer into her hair. I pulled on the wires and two small, round end pieces dropped into her lap. Now she noticed my presence.

"I am sorry. There is so much information here, but a great deal of it is useless. I am trying to make sense of it, to find what is valuable." She rubbed her eyes, looking weary.

I shook my head. *"You must also sleep."*

She smiled, but she did not look happy. *"I am almost finished. I have reviewed thousands of journal articles, newspapers and reports. Very few have noticed the changes we have seen to the ocean's floor. One sees the warmer water temperatures, flowing down this coast, but not the cause. One sees disasters in earthquakes, volcanoes and tsunami, but the focus is on the effect on humans. Several look at changing fish populations and species of birds that eat fish, describing decreasing numbers, but not the reason why. The humans lack perspective."*

I asked the burning question. *"We approach our fishing quota. Do you feel that we have all the information we can yet obtain from the humans?"*

She gave a very human sigh. "No, *I think I must speak to some of the researchers from Fisheries when they are here. I have questions which they may be able to answer. Alternatively, they may need to return to their homes to provide further information. I think we can plan to return to the deeps in less than two weeks. It will be good to swim again. How long have I been working? When will the Fisheries researchers be here?"*

I frowned. Was this a sign of her advanced age? "*You have been working for a solid week, so the researchers will speak tomorrow, but I have told you this already. What are these, and why did you not hear me when I came in?"* I held the wire up, the round end pieces dangling before her face.

"*They are earphones, for music. I developed a taste for it when I studied amongst humans. I have found a new human musical group that did not exist when I was on land before. It is called something about a Machine. Here. Does this not sound like drifting beneath the waves in a storm?"* She pulled the wire out of a hole on the side of the computer and human music filled the house, at considerable volume.

I felt relieved. This was not a mental

instability, after all. *"I understand now why you could not hear me, or the young human fisherman."*

Her face lit with eagerness. *"Joe? Joe came here to look for me, and I missed him?"*

"He looks for you most days. I am sure he will return tomorrow to look for you again," I said reluctantly.

Her response reassured me further. *"I will have finished by tomorrow, aside from speaking to the researchers. Perhaps it will be time to take a rest from working, for a few days only."*

I spoke as a healer must. *"If we must return to the deeps in less than two weeks, a rest will benefit you. You work too hard, Vanessa."*

Vanessa protested my concern, as always. *"I work only as hard as is necessary, to ensure a future for our people and for the humans, even if it is a future I do not live to see."*

I laughed. *"A future you do not live to see? You have perhaps forty more years before a future will occur without you. Have you forgotten that we are not as short-lived as humans?"*

"I do not forget, but I do worry." Her eyes spoke of her age and the depth of her concern.

I looked deep into her ocean-coloured eyes

and let my affection for her colour my tone. *"You worry too much, also. After tomorrow, you must rest."*

She closed her eyes with a nod of acquiescence. *"I think you are correct. I will."*

JOE

"There's some sort of talk up at the Fisheries camp this afternoon. You should come, too," Skipper told me one morning as we walked down the jetty, away from the *Dolphin*.

"Why?" I asked.

"Some changes to the fishing rules out here or something. Fisheries Head Office bureaucrats bringing in some new rules, to justify why they have a job." Skipper shrugged. He evidently didn't like the bureaucrats. "They put on food and tell us what the changes are, so we fish by the rules. That leaves them free to go after the tourists who come out here, ignore the rules and catch too many fish."

"Sure," I replied.

"Head over there around two," he called as he tinkled off down the shingle path.

I had lunch and took the path over to the Fisheries camp. Their camp looked like one of the mining camps I'd helped assemble and rarely got to stay in. A bunch of big dongas, with decking in between. And the new uplink, sticking up where I'd installed it.

I followed the other guys up the decking between two of the buildings and into a room that was obviously the common room of the camp. I saw it all now in daylight. Couches, a huge TV, a commercial-grade kitchen full of gleaming stainless steel and a bunch of dining tables. The tables were pushed up against the wall today, the dining chairs set out in rows behind the sofas. A screen was suspended from the ceiling, next to the TV.

I took one of the dining chairs next to Skipper, who was deep in conversation with the bloke on his other side. The seats were only half full, with plenty of empty chairs. I let my mind drift, hoping I could stay awake through what looked to be a really boring talk.

I was jolted out of my reverie by Vanessa sliding into the chair beside me. "Ooh, have I missed anything?" she asked me with an eager smile.

I smiled in response almost automatically. "They haven't started yet."

"It looks like a big change today – researchers and Head Office staff," Vanessa murmured in my ear.

"Do you know them?" I asked her.

She shook her head. "No, I know some of the senior staff from the Geraldton office. That's Glen, he fancies himself the Lord Mayor of the Abrolhos. I guess he sort of is, in a way. That one's Nick. He's quieter, doesn't say much. That one's Rob, the Geraldton manager. He's not out here much, he can't handle a boat. He is a good cook, though." She pointed at each as she spoke. "Then there's two from Head Office in Perth, plus two from their research office."

"How can you tell which is which?" I asked her.

She pointed at the floor. "From their shoes. All of us are in thongs and sandals, except the office people. They wear closed-in shoes, because they don't like getting their feet wet."

I laughed. "You can't be serious."

She put her hand on my shoulder and leaned closer to point at the offending shoes. "Look. They're the only people in the room who aren't showing their toes. Office staff, of course."

I looked around. Thongs, sandals...and three pairs of closed-in shoes. "What about that one?" I asked, pointing at a third pair of shoes that weren't on the feet of a Head Office person. I looked more closely at the owner of the shoes.

"That's Rob. He's an office person, too."

"Oh." I felt stupid.

She kept her hand on my shoulder for the whole of the talk, her leg brushing mine every time she shifted, occasionally murmuring comments in my ear. My heart beat faster than usual, probably because she was so close.

After the talk finished, Skipper noticed Vanessa next to me. "Are you trying to steal my new lucky deckie, Vanessa? Now I've finally got a deckie who can tell one end of a cray from the other you're going to entice him away to the *Siren*?" He sounded annoyed, but only half serious. He wasn't immune to her smile.

One end of a cray from the other? Yeah, one end'll snap my fingers and toes off and the other end has beady eyes, watching to see if I'm stupid enough to get my fingers or toes within reach. But if she wants to entice me anywhere, all she has to do is ask.

Vanessa laughed. "I wouldn't dare steal your deckie, Skipper, even if he does have a thorough knowledge of anatomy." *God, what I'd give for a more thorough knowledge of her anatomy.* "But I might want to borrow him when the girls go over to Geraldton to do the shopping, if you can spare him."

"For you, Vanessa, anything," Skipper replied. "Just as long as you bring him back in one piece."

Great. Now he's loaning me out like I'm a wheelbarrow. Do I have any say here?

I glanced at Vanessa. To my surprise, she was smiling at me.

"Excuse me, gentlemen, but I want to ask a question." She pressed my shoulder as she stood up, her eyes focused on someone across the room. She took something from the table where the food was and popped it in her mouth as she went past, not breaking stride.

My eyes weren't the only ones watching her cross the room. Heads turned to follow her, all of the faces carefully expressionless. As she stopped beside the Fisheries staff, the same heads snapped back to where they'd been before she moved.

You don't have a hope in hell. None of us do, and deep down we all know it. But we all wish we're wrong.

She greeted a Fisheries researcher with her eager smile and the two were soon in earnest discussion. The researcher pulled up a slide that showed a map of the Western Australian coast, with shifting colours across the ocean. I'd seen it during the talk, but not been interested enough to tune in to the commentary that went with it. Evidently Vanessa had paid more attention than I had.

I turned to the food and piled some up on a plate. I took it to a seat where I had a good view of both her and the rest of the room. The other fishers and deckies descended on the food, too. I heard the door bang and looked out the window to see who'd left without eating. Vanessa's deckies were walking stiffly down the decking toward her boat, as equally deep in conversation as their skipper.

I looked at Vanessa again. She'd finished talking to the researcher and she'd moved on to the Geraldton Fisheries staff. She said a few words and collected smiles from all of them. One of them mentioned the food, pointing at the table. She laughed and walked with Rob, the one with the shoes, to the tables where the food was laid out. She accepted a plate from him and selected a few items from different platters, as he pointed to them.

She moved away from the table, still talking to him. He offered her a drink, which she accepted, balancing the cup and plate somewhat awkwardly. He made some comment that she found funny. When she laughed, she tipped the drink and spilled some on the floor. Rob jumped back quickly, so he didn't get his feet wet.

Trying hard not to laugh, she looked away from him. Her eye caught mine and she flashed me a brilliant smile.

My head went hazy. *Sure I have a say in whether she gets to borrow me. And what I'll say will be, "For you, Vanessa, anything." Joe the wheelbarrow, at your service.*

BELINDA

"You will head to Geraldton tonight or first thing in the morning to replenish supplies. You may return early next week, as you please." Vanessa's voice came from the jetty, as she stepped aboard.

Maria was the first to reply. *"I thought we didn't need supplies until next week? This is a sudden change of plans."*

Vanessa's tone brooked no argument. *"I would like some more fruit: we have only a few raspberries remaining."*

Maria was deferential. *"Do we take the vessel, or did you have some other means of transportation in mind?"*

"I will not accompany you, so the vessel will remain

with me. You may go by air or sea, as you please. There is one more flight this evening, if you wish, with return flights every day this week. The carrier boat departs in the morning for Geraldton and will return in three days," Vanessa said curtly.

Maria's eyes widened with alarm. *"Fly, in a tin tube in the sky? I think not. I would rather swim."*

Vanessa's tone was patient, but no less firm. *"You may travel to Geraldton as you wish, but you must return with human transportation, accompanying the supplies. I recommend you return with the carrier boat. If you miss the boat, you will fly in a human aircraft."*

Remembering her need for rest, I suggested, *"Why do you not accompany us, with the boat? I can never recall your preference in ice cream. Are you staying so that you may assess the performance of the young human fisherman? Surely he can wait until you are rested."*

Her face reddened as she spoke. *"His employer is running the carrier boat this week, as the usual skipper is down in Perth. Skipper decided on my advice to take the carrier boat crew and not his usual deckhand. The young human fisherman has a few days off, with no fishing. I would like to engage in some recreational fishing and water sports with him, for which I will require the vessel. You may enjoy yourselves in Geraldton as you please."*

I relaxed as I realised she would take a break from her work, with or without us. *"We will leave tonight once it is fully dark and enjoy a long swim. We will return with the carrier boat. Likewise, enjoy your water sports."*

JOE

I slept until after the sun was up, for the first time in a month. It felt good to wake up in daylight. I made myself a coffee and took it outside. I stood on the veranda in my shorts, sipping from the chipped mug, looking out over the anchorage as I thought about what I might do today.

I didn't see Vanessa in the shade of her veranda, so her voice startled me.

"Good morning, sleepyhead," she teased. "Did Skipper decide to leave without you?"

"Yep. He's taken the carrier boat back to Geraldton and won't be back till Monday. At the last minute, he decided he only wanted the carrier boat crew and he didn't need me after all. I don't have any electrical jobs scheduled yet, because no one but you knows that I'm not in Geraldton. I get the whole weekend off," I told her, as I stepped onto the path, squinting into the deep shade on her veranda.

She was sitting on a deck chair, wearing a tiny pair of blue shorts and a t-shirt that hugged every curve of her torso perfectly. A steaming mug was on the table beside her, a heavy book in her hands. As I approached, she closed the book and put it down on the table. I turned to read the title: *Anderson's Fairy Tales*. A children's book of short stories. I'd expected her to read something off the adults' bestseller list, which all seemed to be about magic, myths and monsters. Not a book for children.

Grabbing her mug, she joined me on the path, interrupting my thoughts. "That makes two of us, then. The girls went back to Geraldton last night to do some shopping. They said not to expect them till Monday afternoon, but they promised to bring me back some ice cream." She lifted her mug and clinked it against mine. "To a whole weekend off with ice cream at the end of it!" Her nose disappeared into the mug as she drained the contents.

I laughed. "I'll drink to the weekend, but I'll only drink to ice cream if you'll share it with me."

She didn't even hesitate. "It's a deal."

I took a sip of my coffee and we both looked out over the anchorage in silence for a few seconds. The water was almost calm, a phenomenon I'd heard about but never seen.

"So, what are you planning to do with your weekend off?" she asked casually.

I wished I'd planned something thrilling so I could invite her to join me, but since Skipper had told me late last night that I wasn't going to Geraldton all I'd done was sleep and dream of her. "I haven't decided yet," I hedged. "What did you plan to do?"

Her face lit up. "I wanted to go up to the reefs in the Wallabi Group and snorkel some of the dive trails. The girls were talking about some superb fishing spots up there, too." She looked almost embarrassed. "But I can't go up there by myself. I'll need someone to go with me, to help me to handle the boat. Did you want to come?"

I hesitated, dying to spend the day with her but worrying about how I was going to manage that without putting my foot in my mouth or making her regret ever inviting me in the first place.

She mistook my hesitation for unwillingness. "I'll do most of the work. All you'll have to do is help me tie up and untie the boat, and watch the controls if I go to the toilet. You don't have to go in the water, or bait up a line if you don't want to. I'll even cook you dinner, whatever we catch." She clasped her mug to her chest, pausing to take a breath. "Please?"

My eyes had followed the mug and I was having difficulty pulling them away from the front of her t-shirt. I closed my eyes briefly, then lifted my head to focus on her face. She looked worried.

I smiled and was honest. "I'd love to. I haven't snorkelled here before and I've heard it's really good. I'll even clean and fillet the fish, if you cook them."

Her face lit up with a smile. She jumped, bouncing a little, then suddenly hugged me. Before I could respond in kind, she jumped back again. "You are a legend! This will be fun." She took another step away from me, toward her house. "Let me know when you're ready and we'll go." She turned and went inside the house.

I hurried back to my house, slurping the coffee as fast as I could. I barely felt it burning my tongue and the back of my throat.

I dug out my snorkelling stuff from the bottom of my bag. I grabbed some boardshorts and a couple of towels. I dumped the lot on the dining table, heading for the bathroom, and scanned the shelves for the sunscreen. It was next to an unopened box of condoms, which had been sitting there untouched since I arrived. I hesitated, then snatched both up and took them to the kitchen. *You never know, I might get lucky.*

I stuffed the mess on the table into my old backpack. I opened the box of condoms and shoved a few in my pocket. I stuck the rest in the backpack. The chances of any of them getting used were less than me winning lotto, but I figured the chances of me getting any action *without* them were pretty much zero. *Sex tickets. You had to be in it to win it.*

I went back to the bedroom to find a shirt. I had exactly one clean one. I put it on and bundled the remaining ones into the washing machine. I'd do a load of washing when I got back.

Slinging my backpack over one shoulder, I went outside for the fishing gear on the veranda. I grabbed the first packet of bait I saw in the outside freezer, picked up the tackle box and the rods and headed for Vanessa's jetty.

I stowed the gear on the deck of her boat, which looked a lot neater and cleaner than Skipper's.

Siren, it said on the side, in dark blue letters next to the boat number.

I strode down her jetty to her front door, knocking nervously. She opened it almost immediately, smiling.

"I'll be right out," she said, turning to snatch up a bottle of water before stepping outside, closing the door behind her. She carried nothing but the bottle.

She must have noticed me looking, because she smiled again, telling me, "All the rest of my gear is on board already."

She led the way, almost skipping down the jetty. She climbed aboard effortlessly, like any of the other experienced guys, except that she didn't look like one of the guys in those tiny shorts and snug t-shirt.

She glanced at the mess I'd left on her deck as I climbed onto the boat behind her.

"You can stash your dry stuff in the cabin below." She pointed at the door to the main cabin. "Anything you don't mind getting wet can stay out here on deck."

"What about the bait?" I asked.

She kicked the icebox on deck. "In here."

She opened the door to the cabin. I dropped the bait in the icebox and followed her in.

Shit, this is a nice boat. Inside the cabin, level with the deck, was a kitchen almost as big as the one back in my camp on Rat. Next to it was a table with plush bench seats around it.

"Put your stuff downstairs, in the sleeping quarters," she told me, nodding her head toward the stairs. She leaned over to put her water bottle in the fridge.

I tore my eyes from her shorts to watch where I was going. The metal stairs were steep, but the accommodations were surprisingly comfortable. Tiered bunks to sleep twelve, full-length lockers with mirrors and soft carpet on the floor.

"The girls use the bunks at the far end, so dump your gear on any of the bunks closest to the stairs," Vanessa called down.

I dropped my backpack on the nearest and ran back up the stairs, two at a time.

She smiled impishly. "Help me get the boat out of the anchorage and then you can help yourself to anything you like in the fridge. You can watch the satellite TV, if you like, or come up top with me."

She said it like there was a choice.

Where else would I be, but up top with you?

Together, we cast off and she manoeuvred the boat into the anchorage channel. She said little, her expression tense and watchful until we were in the open water of Middle Channel, between the Easter Group and the Wallabis.

When the multicoloured water of the Easter Group had shifted to the solid blue of the channel, she breathed a sigh of relief and turned to me, a little hesitantly. "Could you go down to the kitchen and get me a Pepsi from the fridge? Please get a drink for yourself, too."

"Sure," I replied, climbing down the ladder to the deck. When I looked in the fridge, I saw diet soft drinks, beer and very little else to drink. *Definitely a girl's fridge.* I pulled out her Pepsi and behind it was a carton of iced coffee. I hadn't had an iced coffee since I landed on the islands. *Brilliant.* I shoved them into the pockets of my shorts and headed back up the ladder to Vanessa.

Up on the fly bridge, she bumped her can against my milk carton. "To a fun weekend off!" Her eyes shone, she was so transparently happy.

I returned her smile. "To a fun weekend off," I echoed fervently, hoping she was right.

BELINDA

On our swim between the islands and Geraldton, we met a humpback whale. She told us of sharks who had followed her and we drove them away. Unless a shark is determined on a meal, our people have always been able to make them obey. It was part of the ocean's gift, the ability to sing up all the creatures in the water and to sing them away, too.

In thanks, the whale cow told us of the changes she had seen, to ice in the south and the sea bed to the south and the north. She spoke of the humans in boats who still hunted her kind, though these were less now than in the past we all remembered. She described humans in vessels who came to her simply to watch her swim.

We agreed with her that human behaviour seemed very strange, with some hunters and some admirers. We told her that the humans did not know of the changes to the sea bed, though some knew of changes to the ice.

"Perhaps this will mean the end of the humans. It is sad to lose a species, but life is fleeting." With these parting words, she turned north, heading for warmer waters. She sought a male of her kind, so that she could do her duty. This would be the first year in many that I would not be assisting with the birthing of whale calves in the north. Perhaps next year I would assist in the birth of her calf.

We wished her a safe journey and a strong child.

Her words lingered in my mind as we swam east, toward the mainland. If changing oceans meant the end of humans, what would become of us? There are no males of our kind, which is why we are dependent on humans for our children. Without human males, our people could die out.

I understood in part what drove Vanessa to protect the humans. Without them, even our own people were lost.

JOE

When we sighted the Wallabis, I went downstairs to change into my board shorts. I left my clothes on the bunk beside my backpack.

We moored the boat near one of the dive trails.

"Okay, I'll get changed and then we'll go see some fish!" she called as she climbed down the ladder.

As she hit the deck, she peeled off her shorts and pulled off her t-shirt, to reveal a light blue bikini and plenty of bare skin. *My God.* My mouth must have hung open for a full minute, or long enough for her to take her clothes to the bunkroom and reappear in front of me on the main deck. Her perfect boobs bounced with every step, clearly visible in the skimpy bikini that barely restrained them.

She put on her mask, snorkel and fins and balanced on the edge. She turned to me, winked, and said, "Let's get wet!" Then she vanished over the side.

I struggled into my gear and followed her, more clumsily.

We swam around reefs, rocks and wrecks that all seemed to blend into one another. There were lobsters, coral, seaweed, fish and plenty of other things I didn't know the names of. But Vanessa did – each time she surfaced, she told me more names than I could remember. When I got sick of looking at marine life, there was always Vanessa, gliding through the water almost like a fish herself.

"Did you see the clownfish?" she asked excitedly, as she surfaced for what felt like the hundredth time.

I had no idea. I'd seen lots of fish. Rather than show my ignorance, I asked her the burning question. "How do you know so much about fish? You know the names of everything!"

She laughed. "I studied marine biology in Perth. I finished my degree around six years ago."

She has a perfect body, so of course she's smart, too. She doesn't need anything else to make her utterly unattainable, but she has it anyway. As if I need to be reminded she's so far out of my reach, just being beautiful.

"C'mon, I'll show you the clownfish." She put her snorkel back in her mouth, waiting for me to do the same. Her cool fingers wrapped around my arm, pulling me through the water to the anemones.

After she had pointed out the clownfish, we climbed back aboard to shift the boat to one of the fishing spots. We tied the boat up at the new mooring and she was already in the water before I'd even picked up my mask and snorkel.

I hadn't been in the water very long before she announced it was time to start fishing. It was evening by then and the sun was approaching the western horizon. She climbed out of the water, but when I started to follow her, she shook her head.

"Can you scout around and find me a good place to drop my hook in?" she asked. "See if you can find a nice fish for dinner?"

"Sure." I shrugged and started circling the boat. I quickly found a good section of reef, with some big fish that looked suitable. I surfaced and pointed it out.

Whilst I'd been swimming, she'd been baiting up. I got out of the way as she cast the line out, swimming around to the other side of the boat. We were near a beach, where some seals were lying. I was reaching for the boat ladder again, when I saw a seal leap out of the water, not far from me. Another smaller one did the same on my other side. Swimming with seals was something else I'd never done before.

"Hey, do you want me to come help you catch dinner, or can I swim with the seals for a bit?" I asked her.

She looked over at me. "They're sea lions, not seals, but go for it. I'm sure I can catch dinner while you swim."

I was entranced by the sea lions, which were so agile in the water and in the air it was hard to believe they were the same animals as the comatose ones on the beach. They swam, turned and leaped faster than I could have believed possible. They swam close enough to touch, but they darted away before I could stretch out a hand to make contact. I lost track of the time, I was having so much fun.

All of a sudden the sea lions disappeared. One second they were there, then they were gone. The sun had set and it was starting to get dark, so I headed back to the boat. "Hey, Vanessa," I called. "The sea lions just vanished. Did you see where they went?"

She was standing at the filleting table at the side of the boat, a big industrial plastic apron tied over her bikini, cleaning her catch. She lifted the big filleting knife from the fish as she turned to me.

All of a sudden, she ripped off the apron and leaped into the water, the filleting knife still in her hand.

"No, don't!" I shouted as I saw the fin on top of the water, right beneath her. I swam for the boat as fast as I could. When I reached the ladder, I saw blood in the water, but she was nowhere in sight. I couldn't see the shark, either.

The seagulls chose that moment to claim the fish she'd left on the filleting board, fighting over it on the deck. I scrambled up the ladder in record time, whacking at the gulls with my fins. They left the remains of the fish on the deck, but most of it was gone.

I heard dolphin sounds and a splash, so I went to the side, but I couldn't see her, or the source of the blood. Just that there was a hell of a lot of it.

BELINDA

In the shopping centre, I saw many human children with their parents, reminding me of my own daughter. The human children carried bags strapped to their backs. One particularly small child had a bag almost as big as her body.

A flash of pink caught my eye. On the side of the child's bag was a piece of pink plastic, perhaps the size of the child's hand. It was cut in the shape of a stylised mermaid, a human image of one of our people. The human images covered the creature's chest with clothing. Our people do not like the feeling of fabric between our skin and the water.

The thought of fabric in the water reminded

me of the pink ribbons on Vanessa's crates.

"Excuse me!" I called after the child and the human woman I presumed was her mother.

Both turned to look at me. I hurried toward them.

"Please," I addressed the woman, "could you tell me where you bought the pink tag on her bag?"

I pointed at the mermaid, my voice breathless.

The child smiled at me. "You like my mermaid?" she asked in her chirpy voice.

I missed Zerafina so much my heart ached. "My little girl would love it," I replied.

Her mother cleared her throat. "I ordered it online, with some labels for her school things. Search for school labels, bag tags or name labels. There's lots of companies that do it, plus they deliver to your house."

"Thank you!" I smiled at the mother and child.

They walked off. The child waved and smiled at me over her shoulder.

I resolved to tell this to Vanessa on our return. We would attach mermaids to her crates, a far better idea than her pink fabric strips.

I wondered about the strips, which brought my thoughts to the fisherman. I wondered if his taste for water sports was as great as hers.

JOE

I waited for what felt like forever before Vanessa surfaced near the ladder, throwing the knife back on the deck. I rushed to the side, reaching down to help her up. She felt like a dead weight, I could barely pull her up at all.

Yet she laboriously climbed the ladder, almost reaching the top before I saw she had a sizeable tail clenched in one hand.

"Quick, get the winch around this. I want it out of the water before the blood attracts any more," she panted.

Together, we got a rope tied around the tail and winched its owner aboard. As the bastard came up, my jaw dropped again. It was a tiger shark, maybe three or four metres long, with its head half hacked off, presumably with the filleting knife.

I looked at her in amazement and noticed that her pale bikini top was covered in blood. "Shit, are you okay?" I asked, checking her for bite marks. It took a few seconds before I realised that I had my hands on those amazing boobs and there wasn't a bite or scratch mark on them.

"I'm fine," she reassured me, stepping away to the side, out of reach.

I looked down at the deck, red-faced. "I'm sorry, the sea gulls got your groper." I nudged the remains of the fish with my foot.

She picked up the fish by its tail and sighed. "Damn, I was really looking forward to dinner with the groper." She threw the fish back into the ocean. The head fell off before it hit the water, sinking beneath the waves.

She looked like she was trying not to laugh. "It'll be ok. I think we'll have enough fish for dinner without him." She looked at the shark, then down at herself. There was gore in her hair, too. "Could you cut some fillets for dinner while I have a shower? Dinner here made a mess of my new swimsuit." She aimed a kick at the shark with her bare foot. "Throw what you don't want back over the side. With the blood in the water, the carcass will probably be gone by morning."

Great, sharks having a dinner party next to the boat, where I was swimming only a few minutes ago. "I guess so," I replied, trying to keep my voice steady.

She smiled, grabbed her towel off the deck and shut herself in the shower.

It took me a minute to work out what to do with a fish that wouldn't fit on the filleting board, but I got it winched up so the shark hung vertical enough to start slicing it up. The fillets were huge, but I cut them into smaller pieces, before dumping them in a big box from the kitchen. I threw the rest of the shark over the side, then hosed down the deck and the filleting board, before turning the hose on myself for a few seconds. I looked longingly at the shower, but she was still in there, so after one more squirt of cold water I wrapped my towel around my waist, over my dripping shorts, and headed down to my clothes in the bunkroom. I stripped off and wiped myself down with the wet towel, before piling my wet clothes and wet towel together on the floor. I pulled the dry towel out of my backpack and used it to dry myself off.

I picked up my boxer shorts, wishing I'd had the foresight to buy and wear some in black silk, as opposed to the blue cotton ones I was holding. *Like she'll want to see me in them, anyway.*

A sound behind me made me turn around. She was at the bottom of the stairs, her back to me, leaning over to open the drawer under the bunk across from me. She picked a couple of items from the drawer and laid them on the bed. She was close enough to touch, but she hadn't seen me yet. That wasn't what made me freeze, unable to move or speak.

She was naked, her perfectly curved body on full display. Her hair hung down in damp ribbons like seaweed, almost to her luscious arse. Her perfect boobs stood out from her chest above her slightly curved belly, her nipples erect. Every inch of her skin looked smooth and flawless. I itched to reach out and touch her, perhaps a metre from me.

I forced myself to look away, but that didn't help. I could see her amazing body from all angles in the mirrors on the locker doors.

Something blue and lacy in her hands, she moved to stand in front of one of the locker mirrors. She was looking down at first, but she lifted her eyes slowly until it looked like she was scrutinising her own reflected face in the mirror. From where I stood, it looked like her reflection had her eyes on me.

She smiled. "I take it you like what you see." She turned around to face me, looking down. "Impressive."

I looked down and dropped my arms to hold my shorts over where they needed to be. I had the biggest, most painful boner in history from looking at her naked and I'd forgotten that I was starkers, too.

FUCKfuckfuckfuckfuckfuckfuckfuckfuckfuckfuckf uck...

I stared down at my feet, wishing I could sink through the floor.

Then my feet were obscured, by a pair of

dark nipples on the end of two perfect breasts. Cool hands tugged my boxer shorts out of my grasp and tossed them aside. She cupped my hands in hers and placed them around her boobs.

"Fuck," I whispered.

She laughed, her boobs bouncing in my hands. "I'd love to." She touched her lips to mine.

Without knowing how it happened, I was kissing her. Her boobs were soft up against my chest whilst I was hard against her belly. She was pushing me closer to the bunk where I'd left my clothes, sweeping them onto the floor.

I took one hand off her to fumble for the shorts I'd been wearing this morning. I had two fingers in the right pocket, touching the edge of the plastic packaging, before she tried to pull my shorts away.

"I don't think you'll be needing your clothes for a while," she said softly.

I pulled the condoms out of my pocket and threw the shorts on the floor myself. I held the packets up. "I don't want there to be any regrets afterwards." I eased away from her enough to put one of them on, tossing the empty packet and the unused ones onto the highest bunk, within easy reach.

She threw herself at me, tipping us both across the lowest bunk, with her on top of me. She sat up on her knees and teased me for what felt like an interminable amount of time, rubbing against me until I felt her shudder with pleasure more than once.

When I finally slid inside her, it felt incredible, like I never wanted to be out. Time and time again, just before I came, she'd shift and change position, letting the climax build and build until she shifted again. She was driving me insane with want for her.

When she shifted to kneel on top of me again, I fastened my hands over her hips, grinding her against me with each thrust so that she was so focused on her own orgasm she wouldn't shift and delay mine. I heard her breath stutter into short gasps and I increased the pace, so close I could almost taste it. I heard her cry out before I felt her back arch and her body shudder again. In those precious few moments, I came with her, my shout blending with hers. It was mind-blowingly good.

"Damn, that was good," she gasped, her breasts heaving as she tried to catch her breath.

This is too good to be true. It has to be a dream, my most vivid, X-rated, perfect dream ever. I'd better make the most of it before I wake up.

I sat up, feeling her shift as if she were going to move off me. I stuck my arms around her back, crushing her boobs against my chest as I kissed her. I was still hard inside her and I wondered if the second time would be as good as the first. Still panting from Round 1, I wondered if this dream would last long enough to include Round 2. I was definitely up for it.

She disengaged from me gently, rolling off me to flop onto the bunk beside me, still breathing hard. I rolled onto my side, leaning over her to kiss her again.

If she's too exhausted for anything else, missionary style is okay by me. I shifted, ready to roll on top of her and start over.

She started laughing and pushed me off her, rolling me back onto my back. She was up in a crouch, climbing nimbly over my legs to stand on the carpet.

My hopes for Round 2 wilted.

"I want dinner before we do any more. I'm *hungry*." She snatched up something white from the bunk on the other side, pulling it over her head. The filmy cotton dress didn't fit her as tightly as the t-shirt she'd worn earlier, but its transparency made up for that, leaving nothing to the imagination.

Meanwhile, my imagination spun out of control.

She started up the steps. "You go get cleaned up and I'll start dinner. I'm going to need all the energy I can get if you plan more of this tonight." She reached the top and disappeared from view.

More? She wants more. Oh yes, thank you God!

BELINDA

We watched human television programmes and despaired of the humans ever noticing that their world was changing. There was lots of singing, dancing, cooking and house maintenance. There were simplified pictures with simple stories for human children. Maria bored of these quickly and found a channel that played longer movies, with only minimal singing, dancing or cooking.

She watched this for most of the day, as one movie would finish and another would start.

One movie bored her and she changed channels again. This time, the channel was showing a news programme. Humans were killing each other in one country and people from Australia were being killed by the humans from another country where the Australians were dressed in mottled clothing. There were pictures of large numbers of people on small boats, low in the water, wearing life jackets. These people were leaving one country to come to Australia and their vessel was not safe, so humans from Australian vessels were assisting these people to transfer to the Australian vessels and taking them to a camp much like those at the Abrolhos. These camps were in much better repair and not in such bright colours as Abrolhos camps. The programme concluded with a short feature on how a human became injured whilst wearing very small tight shorts and carrying some sort of ball on a grass field, as he collided with another human. This was portrayed as a very grave event.

"They are interested more in their society than the world which permits the society to exist. This may explain why they seem to know so little about the changes to the sea floor that will reshape their lands." Maria's words surprised me.

I tried to defend them, as Vanessa might. *"Perhaps it is simply that they do not know. They have technology to detect the changes; once the humans know, perhaps they will take more interest in changes to more than their society."*

Maria snorted. *"Vanessa is too optimistic. Does she not know that the humans are too preoccupied with themselves to see?"*

"I suspect she knows more of human preoccupations than we ever could. I think she will save our people and theirs as well, if she can," I said fondly.

Maria shook her head. *"What you say is an impossible task that she cannot accomplish."*

"For us perhaps, but not for her," I replied slowly. *"You will see. We will bring our information back to our people and they will send her to obtain more, even as she reports that there is not yet more. On land, she will inspire the humans to find what she needs to ensure the survival of our people. She will even strive to help the humans, if she can."*

Maria was incredulous. *"Why? Is not doing her duty to our people enough?"*

Maria did not know Mother. I tried to explain. *"Not for her. She cares for our people, above and beyond simple duty. I think she cares for the humans, too. It is not in her nature to allow life to be lost when she could save it. Even a human life."*

Maria voiced the dread that we both felt. *"I still feel she works toward an impossible goal in which she cannot succeed."*

I tried to see hope. *"Yet I feel she will succeed, despite our doubts. She understands humans better than any of our kind ever has, yet she is one of our elders. She will accomplish what none of us could. In her own way, she is the ocean's gift to humans, ensuring their survival when their world will be irrevocably changed."*

Maria's shock was written plainly across her face. *"She would reveal the ocean's gift to humans? It is because we are hidden from humans that we survive!"*

I made my voice soothing. *"No, she protects our people above all, above even the humans' interests. You will see."*

The television blared a musical advertisement about a singing and dancing programme that would soon be broadcast. In annoyance, I pressed a button that silenced the sound and bright images. *"I have had enough of what humans consider entertainment. I think we should venture to the hotel bar, consume some alcohol and watch some real humans for entertainment."*

Maria hesitated. *"I do not wish to become drunk. I would prefer one of those cold coffee drinks."*

I agreed and we both left the hotel room to go to the bar downstairs. There were a few humans there, including one behind the bar who sold the drinks. Maria chose a table whilst I went to order drinks.

I had learned that whiskeys varied as much as humans did, and poor whiskey was best with ice to dull the taste. "I would like a whiskey with ice. What do you have that is cold and tastes of coffee?" I asked the man behind the bar.

"We have coffee cocktails," he told me.

I didn't know what he meant, but I asked for two of these and brought all three drinks to the table where Maria was seated. I placed the two coffee ones in front of her and kept the whiskey for myself. We were thirsty and finished our drinks quickly. I ventured to the bar to purchase more

JOE

When I went up the stairs to the main cabin, Vanessa was going through the kitchen cupboards, stretching up to reach the high ones. Her hemline rose tantalisingly to the tops of her legs. I forced myself to look away so I didn't trip on my way to the shower.

I shut the door and hung the towel on the back of it. I turned the shower on and looked around for the soap. Lined up on the soap dish were three bottles of brightly coloured shower gel, but no bar of soap. *A girl's bathroom, all right.*

While the water cascaded down over my body, I examined the bottles. Lavender, sea minerals and pomegranate. I grabbed the sea mineral one, wondering why anyone would want a sea mineral shower when you could just jump over the side and have as many fresh sea minerals as you liked, and lathered up. I washed the foam off, hoping I didn't smell too girly, and towelled myself dry. Wrapping the towel around my waist again, I returned to the bunkroom.

Vanessa was intent on shaking the fillets in a bag half full of something that looked like breadcrumbs. She barely noticed me walk past. I wondered if I should have left off the towel – maybe she would have noticed me then. I hung the damp towel over a spare railing in the bunkroom and looked for my clothes. I found my shorts first – she'd thrown the boxer shorts somewhere – and decided they'd do. *Especially if they're coming off soon for Round 2, after dinner.* Already turned on at the thought, I reached for the condoms on the top bunk and stuck them back in my pocket.

I took the stairs two at a time, then stood by the table. She looked up and smiled, holding out a baking tray full of fish, covered in something that looked like flour flecked with green. "I found some fish batter in the top cupboard, so I covered some of the fillets in that and I'll bake them all together. I also found a mushroom pizza, so I stuck that in the oven, too. Do you think that will be enough?"

"Plenty," I replied. I watched her lean over to put the baking dish in the oven. The white skirt rode up again. It would have revealed the bottom of her underwear, if she'd been wearing any. Instead, I caught a glimpse of pussy between her legs, before she straightened up again. I blinked, trying to hold onto the memory.

Time for a drink, I think. Is there anything stronger than beer? I moved into the kitchen, starting to look through the cabinets. Behind me, Vanessa reached for a sponge in the sink and started cleaning the bench. I found breakfast cereal and a few cans of vegetables, but most of the cupboards were empty. Vanessa's crew must have gone to do the food shopping, too. *Beer it is, then.*

I stood behind her, waiting for her to get out of the way so I could get to the bar fridge under the bench. She finished wiping the bench top and threw the sponge back into the sink. The remaining fillets were still in the box on the draining board, so she spun on the spot to lift up the box, then leaned over to put them in the fridge.

Standing right behind her, I got more than a glimpse this time. The light glistened on her skin, she was still so wet. I couldn't do anything else but stare.

Her head still in the fridge, oblivious, she called over her shoulder, "What would you like to do while we wait for dinner to cook? Would you like me to get you a drink? What do you want?"

She stayed bent over, waiting for my answer, as I was mesmerised by the wet dark cleft between her legs, right in front of me. *What do I want?* "I want to bend you over that bench, drop my shorts and fuck you from behind," I blurted out.

I should have asked for a beer. At least I'd get that.

BELINDA

"These coffee milks make it difficult to think." Maria's words were not entirely clear, but I still understood them.

"Yes, they do," I agreed.

The man who had been behind the bar came to explain to us that the bar would soon be closed, so would we like to order a last drink? I ordered two more for each of us. He brought these to our table and we drank them quickly.

Maria stood up to go and she seemed to have difficulty with her balance. I stood and attempted to support her, but this pushed me off-balance, so that I found walking difficult, too. We chose to go outside of the hotel, to the beach nearby, instead of straight back to our rooms.

"I feel terribly hot and unwell. Are you sure you did not order hot coffee instead of cold?" Maria said, sounding worried.

"The drinks were all cold," I assured her. *"Perhaps you should immerse yourself in the ocean, to better regulate your body temperature."*

"That sounds like a good idea," Maria slurred. She removed her clothes on the beach, walking into the water without them. She took a shallow dive under a wave and I sat down to wait for her, beside the pile of her human clothing. She surfaced almost immediately, clearly still human. *"The coffee drink has taken my tail!"*

I found this amusing and joined her in the water, to demonstrate that she was mistaken. I left my clothes on top of hers on the beach. I ducked under the water and concentrated on my form, willing my legs to join together to form my tail once more. The flow was slower to start, but I could feel my tail flukes lengthening. I savoured the sensation of water flowing over my skin and lost focus. I could see not flukes but feet. I was bewildered.

Maria's words alarmed me. "*I am going to swim to Vanessa and inform her that this drink has taken my tail.*"

Maria dived again, but her form remained human. I dived for her to pull her back, catching her foot. She fought to free herself from me as I fought to retain my hold. If she tried to swim to Vanessa's cursed islands from here in her human form, she would drown like a human. If she managed to shift to her tail and survive the swim, she would interrupt Vanessa's water sports with the young fisherman, in contravention of our orders. I could not permit either of these.

I pulled her into the shallow water, where she gave up, sitting on the sand and letting the waves break over her legs. I sat down beside her.

"Excuse me ladies," an apologetic human male voice said from behind us.

I turned and stood.

The human from behind the bar looked embarrassed and averted his eyes from me.

"It's not a good idea to be out here without your clothes. It's not safe. You really should get dressed and return to your hotel room."

"Thank you, we will," I replied, leaving the water to put my clothes on again. "Maria?" I called.

I heard the man make a wordless exclamation. I turned in concern, to see Maria finish a passionate kiss with the embarrassed human. She left wet streaks down his clothing. "It is a pleasure to meet a kind man," she mumbled.

I snatched up her clothes and caught her arm as she stumbled away from the poor human. I passed her the human clothing she had left on the beach and she struggled to put it on. In the end, I had to help her into her t-shirt and shorts.

Together, supporting each other, we returned to the hotel and our room, where I locked the door behind us. Maria keeled over, face down on her bed, wet as she was.

Her voice was quiet, mumbling and slurred, but I could just discern the words: *"Human men are not all bad."*

I smiled. Our people do not hide anything from one another, but I would like to hide the events of this evening. I hoped Vanessa's water sports were so enjoyable that she did not think to ask us for details of our leisure activities.

Less incapacitated than Maria was, I chose to remove my damp clothes and take a hot shower before I retired. Thanks to the human inventions of hot running water and alcohol, I could not think of a more memorable time.

Except, perhaps, one weekend in the past, which also involved whiskey, with water and fire…

I brought my thoughts back to the present. I can only hope Vanessa will never know of it.

JOE

In my dreams, I heard the dolphins again, distantly, but I ignored them. My dreams were filled with Vanessa. Everything ached from too much swimming and sex yesterday, so I resisted waking for as long as I could, savouring even the thought of her. Oh my God, on the kitchen bench, then the dining table, carpet burns from the floor, those raspberries…

I reached over, to where I was sure she'd slept beside me, but the bunk was cold and empty. The blankets and sheets were made up with almost military precision, I saw in the dim light filtering through the half-closed hatch above.

I looked around for my clothes. They were folded neatly on top of my backpack, in the corner of the floor by the stairs, with my boxer shorts on top.

I dressed and went upstairs to the kitchen. I made myself a cup of black coffee. I'd learned to take my coffee black on my first trip out to site three years ago, as fresh milk and bread were always the first supplies to run out. At the Abrolhos, it was the same. Even Vanessa's organised vessel was not immune to the lack of fresh staples.

Where was Vanessa? This was her boat, moored off an uninhabited island. Where else would she be?

The kitchen was as clean as when I'd stepped aboard yesterday, so she'd certainly been up. A packet of frozen croissants sat on the sink draining board, the cardboard box damp from melted ice.

I heard footsteps on the deck outside, so I left the cabin to stand on the main deck, coffee in hand.

She stood dripping on the main deck,

wearing a fresh, clean bikini in a darker shade of blue. In one hand she held a baldchin groper and in the other a huge rock lobster. "I caught breakfast!" she told me cheerfully. "So, do you want fish, lobster or croissants?"

The lobster snapped his tail menacingly and dropped a leg on the deck. I looked down at the dark red limb.

Lobster for breakfast? Shit, before I came up here I wouldn't have eaten one and now I hate them more than ever.

"Croissants," I answered.

She held up the lobster and glared at him. "YOU can be lunch." She dropped him over the side, back into the water.

Vanessa slapped the fish on the filleting board and started cleaning it. In a very short time, the fish was nicely filleted and she was looking at it thoughtfully.

"I'd like croissants, too," she said, taking the fish into the cabin. "But I don't think we have enough butter for lunch, if we have croissants for breakfast. Do you mind if we head back to Rat in a few hours, so we can be at my house by noon? It looks like the only food we have left on the boat are the fillets from yesterday and today."

"Sure." I shrugged. This bikini was skimpier than the one she'd worn yesterday. It was occupying a considerable share of my attention as she bounced around the kitchen, ripping open the packet of croissants and putting them on a tray in the oven. She set the timer before turning to face me again.

"Thank you so much for coming up to the Wallabis with me!" She wrapped her arms around my neck and hugged me, pressing her body against mine. She was still cold and wet from her swim, so I was a little hesitant about holding her too close. She immediately noticed and took a step back.

"I'm still dripping wet," she apologised. "I should take my wet bathers off and do something about that."

She grabbed a towel from the dining table. My heart leaped and then sank as she headed down to the lower cabin. I sat at the table to wait.

When she came back up again, her t-shirt covered her boobs completely.

The dream's over. At least she was mine for a night. And what an incredible night…

I was startled out of my reverie by the oven timer. Vanessa was already in the kitchen, shifting plates and cutlery around.

She put everything on the dining table in front of me. She sat down across from me and started buttering a croissant for herself.

I shoved half a croissant into my mouth. With my mouth full, it was harder to ask her if I'd ever get to sleep with her again.

She nibbled on the end of one, looking thoughtful. "It's just after eight now. We have two to three hours before we have to head back down to Rat for lunch. Did you want to have another snorkel, or maybe try another fishing spot? If you're still tired from yesterday, you can always go pick a bunk and sleep till then. What would you prefer?"

I'd prefer to pick up where we left off last night. Fuck swimming, snorkelling, fishing or sleep, all I want is you.

I gritted my teeth so I wouldn't say it aloud. Then I took another huge bite of my breakfast.

If you're not going to mention sex, I'm not saying a

word about it. Shit, does that mean she didn't enjoy herself as much as I did last night? I should have taken it more slowly. I've fucked up royally now.

I swallowed the last of my croissant. "Whenever you want to head back to Rat is fine with me. I think I've had enough snorkelling and fishing to last me all weekend."

She smiled, but she didn't look as happy as she had last night. "Sure," she said softly. "We can head back as soon as I'm done with the breakfast dishes."

BELINDA

Maria recalled little of our drunken escapade of the previous evening, remaining in bed as long as she could before we checked out of the hotel. She required human pain-relief medication and remained unwell for a considerable time afterwards.

As we packaged our purchases for transport on the carrier boat, she said little and I said less. I did not want to draw attention to the insanities of last night, or her change of heart toward humans.

Once our purchases were secure aboard the carrier boat, we had time to consume lunch before the vessel departed.

I chose a small shop a short distance from where the boat was moored. This shop sold cooked fish with chips and carried a considerable reputation among the humans for the quality of the fish. In my past experience, I felt this reputation was merited, as the fish was obtained from the fishing boats nearby, so it was fresher than most mainland fish.

Maria said that she was too unwell to consume any human food yet, so I ordered my meal whilst she sat outside the shop, looking at the vessels in the small harbour. The smell of boat fuel was strong, but not strong enough to discourage my taste for food.

Skipper watched us cross the paved parking area from the shop to his vessel. "Ready, girls? All aboard for the Abrolhos!" He grinned widely as he said this.

I permitted a small smile to cross my face in response as I boarded his vessel, followed by Maria.

We were not in the open ocean for long before Maria leaned over the side of the vessel and voided the contents of her stomach. When she was finished, she wiped her mouth and mumbled a commitment to avoid strange human drinks that were both warm and cold.

I smiled and said nothing. I thought of my whiskey, carefully packed in with our supplies. I would miss the fiery drink when we returned to the deeps, but I still had a week left in which to enjoy it.

JOE

The southerly was in, so it was pretty choppy in Middle Channel. We made it halfway across before she suddenly turned to me and asked me to take over.

She almost slid down the ladder and stumbled to the side before she threw up. And again. And again...

She hugged the side of the boat until we were in the anchorage. She straightened up to help me tie up at her jetty, her face pale.

"What's wrong? Are you ok?" I asked, worried.

She smiled wanly. "I get seasick. Thank you for getting us back safely."

I found this hilarious. "Seriously, you get seasick?" *Even the perfect woman has a flaw.*

"Yes." She sounded resigned and looked shaky as she held on to one of the canopy posts for support.

I unloaded my gear onto the jetty, then jumped down after it. "Do you need a hand?" I asked doubtfully, offering it anyway.

She smiled again, shaking her head. "No, I'll just tidy up here a little bit, then I'll head back to my place and make a start on something for lunch. Don't want my deckhands complaining about me having orgies on their boat while they're away." She pulled a face.

I forced a laugh and loaded myself up with gear. "Thanks for a fun weekend off. I haven't enjoyed myself this much in a long time." *Like ever.*

She looked rueful. "It's been ages since I had such a good time, too. Hey, the weekend's not over yet. You're welcome to join me for lunch, if you'd like."

"Yeah, sure," I replied.

I lugged my fishing and snorkelling gear down her jetty, toward my house. Just as I set foot on the path, one of the guys from Southern Group emerged from my veranda.

"You're Joe, the sparky who's deckying for Skipper this season, right?" he asked me, looking desperate.

"That's me," I said easily, dropping the rods on the veranda. I started to hang up my towels and boardies over the rope clothes line.

"The big generator on Basile's blown and we need to get it fixed. We've got freezers full of stuff defrosting, and if we need to get any parts from Gero, we'll need to know before tomorrow so we can get them on a plane or the carrier boat..." he babbled.

"Sure, I'll come take a look," I told him. "Let me get my tools. Did you bring a boat? I've only got my tinny."

"Of course. I'll give you a lift down, you can stay the night in one of the empty deckie camps, we'll feed you and bring you back in the morning. Let me know what parts you need and we'll radio the mainland to send it out tomorrow." He stood there on my veranda, waiting.

I dumped my snorkelling gear on the

veranda by the door and went in. I looked for a clean shirt and didn't find any, so I went to the laundry and set off a load in the washing machine. I picked up my toolbag and headed out.

"Right, to Basile Island," I told him.

Vanessa stepped off her jetty as we started down the path to where he'd moored his boat. *She's like a dream I want to keep having, but I have to wake up and go to work.*

"I'm sorry," I told her. "Generator's blown on Basile in the Southern Group. I'll grab some lunch down there. I'll be back tomorrow some time."

She smiled and nodded. "Some of the best food on the islands is cooked on Basile. Hell, I'd take their cooking over mine any day. Good luck with their generator. See you when you get back."

The bloke from Basile and I watched her walk down the path, go inside her house and close the door, before either of us said anything else.

"She invited you over for lunch?" he asked, leading the way to the boat.

"Yeah. We both had a weekend off, so we went up to the Wallabis to do some snorkelling and fishing while her crew is over in Geraldton. She needed a hand to handle the boat." I tried to sound casual as I followed him, trying not to think of what else she'd let me handle.

"Catch anything good?"

"A shark and a couple of gropers." I made it sound offhand. *Don't ask how big the shark was, or what else we did. I'm still not sure I wasn't dreaming.*

We both climbed onto his boat, where he and the other crewman cast off. We cruised along the anchorage.

Vanessa was on her veranda, taking down some washing. She waved and smiled as we went past.

"You're playing with fire with that one," the bloke from Basile warned me.

"She seems real sweet and friendly to me," I replied. *So friendly she spread her legs for me...*

"It's your funeral, mate," the other bloke chimed in.

Well, it was a quiet trip to Basile Island after

that.

BELINDA

We were the only passengers Skipper carried on his carrier boat. The vessel pounded across the waves, jarring my teeth and bones. Oh for swimming beneath the waves, the smooth flow through water…

When the islands came into view, they first appeared to be more waves on the horizon. As we approached, the browns and greens of the prostrate vegetation on the uninhabited islands made them distinguishable from waves, as the white sands blended into white foam. I could discern sea lions sleeping on the shores of these islands, secure in their isolation. Some of them were much smaller than the somnolent creatures they lay closest to, and I knew these were the juveniles, lying beside their mothers. Like our kind, the males did not remain long with the mothers and the mothers protected their own.

I thought of Zerafina, who would enjoy a swim with these sea lions, or the dolphins we played with by night. One day, when she was old enough to swim the great distances across oceans, I would take her here. We would swim with dolphins and sea lions, through coral gardens and algal forests. I knew my sisters in the deep would protect her and care for her until I returned, but I missed her still.

I looked out across the waves, which were smaller now that we were inside the Easter Group. The anchorage was in view, with the houses like coloured boxes lined up along the eastern shore. This would be the last time I would travel this way by boat. Our fishing was complete and our fishing for information neared completion, too.

I will be home soon, my Zerafina. I have such stories to tell you, of humans and dolphins, sea lions and stars.

JOE

The guys from Basile dropped me off at Rat before dawn, before they went to check their pots. They didn't want me to see their fishing spots, I gathered, though I didn't much care.

I nodded goodbye as their boat disappeared into the darkness, my pocket full of cash and a carton of beer in my arms. I'd fixed the generator, then rewired most of the houses on the island. *If I get many more days like this, I'm going to buy Dean a beer. I'd never made so much money on holidays before.*

I walked slowly back to my place, dropping the beer off on the veranda. There was plenty in the fridge. I wouldn't need these for a while.

I went over to Vanessa's place, but all the lights were out. As it was the early hours of the morning and she wasn't fishing until her crew returned in the afternoon, she was probably fast asleep. I left without knocking on the door.

With a sigh, I trudged home to my place and went to bed alone to dream about her, a poor substitute for the real thing.

BELINDA

The wheelbarrow was loaded with the human food from the mainland and pushed to the vessel. We unloaded it on deck, before Maria returned for a second load.

Vanessa and I shifted the food from the deck to the various refrigerated storage cabinets on the vessel, to give Maria space to unload the next wheelbarrow-load.

I noticed the smell as I stepped into the cabin, a smell I had not known since I did my duty for Zerafina. My shock was complete. She hadn't just touched the young human, she had joined with him. From the strength of the smell, she had done this many times. I was as speechless as the young human fisherman, before I stiffly spat out the words. *"So you had fun with the young human fisherman."*

Her response was calm. *"I certainly enjoyed my time with him."* She looked at the food she was packing into the deep freeze unit and not at me.

I took my small bag of clothing down into the bunkroom. The smell was stronger here. I started to put my clean clothes away and collect the soiled clothes in the laundry hamper. In the hamper already were some of her and my clothing, all of it rich with the smell of sex. I lifted up my human swim clothing from the hamper, to find it discoloured with blood. I swayed, disoriented. She had enjoyed this human as much as I had enjoyed the man with whom I did my duty.

I marched up the steps to the main cabin, bringing the ruined swim clothing with me. *"Is there anywhere on this vessel that you did not enjoy him? His smell is all over the kitchen and the bunkroom. I will be unable to rest with his smell permeating the whole vessel,"* I hissed.

Vanessa sounded disinterested. *"You can*

clean the vessel if his smell offends you."

I held up the bloody human swim clothing. "*What of this? It will resist cleaning.*"

She glanced up, before her attention returned to the deep freeze unit. "*Oh, a shark tried to attack him. I was wearing your swim clothing at the time and I did not have time to remove it. The human was unharmed. The shark fillets are in the deep freeze, here, if you would like some.*"

I dismissed the offer. "*Shift them to the house refrigeration units. Our fish quota is caught and both Maria and I wish to return home. We will not crew the vessel past this week. We have made arrangements for its storage.*"

She turned to face me. "*And if I am not ready to leave?*"

"*You can stay and dally with the human fisherman for as long as it pleases you. But we shall not. I wish to return to my daughter and Maria is impatient to return to the deep.*" In my anger, my voice was bitter.

Vanessa's voice held a warning. "*We must depart together, and I lead this group, not you.*"

I ignored the warning and said words I would later regret. "*We have a duty to return to our people with the information we have obtained. Mating with human males is not part of our duty for this trip, or has your memory become clouded with time? If so, it is time to step down as elder and appoint your successor. Either Maria or I will take pleasure in fulfilling your role as elder, but in that case we must return to the deep immediately for the appointment to be agreed upon by the other elders."*

I felt angry that her actions had surprised me, so I made a threat I knew was empty. She could not step down as elder until her work was complete. It seemed so incongruous, then, that she should indulge the urges of this human when she had far more pressing matters to attend to.

"No, my memory has no clouds. Only bright sunlight, mystery under the stars and the currents deep beneath the surface. I shall sate myself and return with you to the deep, soon. Do you not remember when you enjoyed the time you spent with a human man?"

Her calm, assured response only served to anger me further.

"Not at present. It appears I have a vessel to clean and sanitise, and a large quantity of clothing and linen to wash, before Maria is also sickened by the nauseating smell pervading it all. If you choose to offer

your body to the human fisherman again, please confine your activities to the house and your own human clothing.'' I stalked to the sleeping cabin, where I quickly stripped all the linen from the beds and placed it in the hamper. I heaved the full hamper up the stairs and across the deck to the jetty.

As my furious footsteps sounded on the jetty, made heavier by the load I carried, I reflected briefly on her words. *"No, I do not wish to remember the time I spent with a human man when the time spent in remembrance is time I do not share with Zerafina. My fiery daughter, from those warm nights in the arms of a human. Time spent with her is far more precious than any brief dalliance with a human man, however warm and pleasurable his embrace. Even a human who washes frequently."*

I did not know if she heard my words, but I also did not care.

JOE

The sun was barely above the horizon and Vanessa was already hanging out her washing, her back to me. Today she wore red and it made her look thinner, somehow. I hoped she hadn't been really sick, instead of just slightly seasick.

I approached her as quietly as I could, just watching her.

"Good morning," I greeted her with a smile.

She turned as if I'd hit her, and I realised my mistake. "It might be, if the southerly would calm down some." Her voice was colder than her icy expression.

"You're not Vanessa," I stammered.

"No," she replied frostily. "*I* am Belinda, deckhand on the *Siren*." She said this as though she were announcing her appointment as the queen of the known universe, instead of telling me she was just a deckie, the same as me.

I bit back a laugh. The ice queen might have delusions of grandeur, but I didn't want to get into a fight with Vanessa's deckie. "Where is she?" I asked reasonably. Hell, if I'd met this one first, I wouldn't have come within shouting distance of any of the crew of the *Siren*. Belinda looked like she could have taken Vanessa's dinner shark with nothing but her teeth before using me for a toothpick.

"The *Siren* is moored at her jetty," Belinda said slowly, as if to an idiot, before she turned and pointed at the boat.

"Not the bloody boat. Vanessa. Where's Vanessa?" I asked, getting irritated.

"She's making arrangements for the *Siren* to go into storage until next season, so that we can leave by Monday." She sniffed with distaste.

"Vanessa's leaving next Monday?" I blurted out.

"If I can't persuade her to leave any sooner, yes." Unwilling to prolong the conversation any further, Belinda the ice queen turned on her heel and stalked up the jetty back to Vanessa's boat.

I stuck my tongue out at the sourpuss's back. Now that I looked more closely, I saw the differences. Belinda was thinner, with much smaller boobs. She walked more stiffly than Vanessa, as if each step required a conscious effort. Or she had a spare fishing rod up her arse. Add that to her expression and she was such a different girl, I wondered why Vanessa put up with her.

Maybe she cleans the boat like a demon. Or maybe she makes ice between her legs to fill the icebox. I started laughing and found I couldn't stop.

Belinda turned and glared at me, almost tripping over and falling into the water. She straightened up in an air of high dudgeon, her nose in the air, as she trotted back to the *Siren.*

BELINDA

Vanessa observed me in conversation with the human and she waited unhappily for my return to the vessel. *"I asked you to avoid contact with the young human fisherman."*

I felt defensive. Had she not observed that he initiated the conversation with me?

Her eyes were still on the human, through the cabin window. *"You gave him information that saddened him. I would have preferred to do this in a kinder manner than you did."*

I closed my eyes. I forced the words out, hoping that I wouldn't have to put them into action. *"It was not my intention to hurt the human. I will return and apologise to him, if you wish."*

Her voice was firm and commanding. "*I do not. I would like you to avoid contact with him, particularly now. Our time here is limited, and I must make amends for your rudeness.*"

Swiftly, she crossed the deck and climbed off the vessel to stand on the jetty. The human's face lit up as she approached him. I watched them and listened to the conversation that the wind carried across the anchorage.

She greeted him with a smile. "Good morning, Joe."

He was more abrupt. "Good morning. Your deckie said you're leaving next week."

"Yes, with the fishing season finishing, I've filled my quota. At the end of the season, it's time to return home, until next year," she told him gently. "Skipper plans to leave not long after I do. He's had a good season, too."

He seemed to have difficulty speaking. "But I thought you'd stay until the end of the season, at least until the end of next week, when I go back to the mining camps…"

"I'd like to stay longer, but I must go home," she said softly. Her hand dropped to her stomach, which now had a slight curve to it that I had not noticed before.

Did the human food make her swell in the middle? Surely not. She did not eat a great deal.

At first, I dismissed the other possible reason. She had joined with the human only a few days ago, it was too soon for her to be changing if she were carrying the human's child. It was far too early to tell, unless…

Unless she joined with him the night we rescued him from the rock? That night was four weeks in the past, sufficient time for her to know if she carried a child. A child would explain why she was so willing to return with us, to ensure she was in the deeps as the child grew within her until it was time to birth her at the Nursery Grounds.

"Come in and have some breakfast. The girls brought some eggs and I've been dying for some scrambled eggs…" Vanessa took the human's hand and led him into her house.

Strong preferences for certain foods and strong emotional responses, both tell-tale signs of carrying a child. My suspicions grew.

JOE

I talked her into going to the community club on Little Rat for a drink with the rest of us. It was her last night for the season, and she'd never been.

"I have been to the club, plenty of times before you arrived," she responded, stung.

I'd forgotten that she'd been here before I arrived. It was hard to believe she was more a part of this place than I was. It had grown on me, like some horrible fungal disease.

"I'm sorry. It's just that I've never seen you there." I hesitated, not sure what else to say. I chose honesty. "It's the last chance I'll get to have a drink with you in the club, before you leave in a few days. I'm only here for the season and I'll probably be back at the mines soon. Just one evening and I'll buy you a drink."

Her expression softened. "Okay, I'll come and you can buy me a farewell drink, but we're taking my dinghy and I'm driving it."

Shit. She'd noticed the dents in my dinghy, too.

"Sure," I replied. *Yes!*

"Let me get a clean shirt on, then I'll be ready to go." She vanished into her house.

I should probably get some clean clothes on, too. I ducked back into my shack.

I put on my least stained pair of shorts and the polo shirt that seemed destined to be The Last Clean Shirt. I'd worn this on her boat more than a week ago, when we went fishing up in the Wallabis, and not worn it since. I shoved some condoms in my pocket, praying that I'd get to use one tonight.

It took her twenty minutes longer than me to find a clean shirt. The one she chose was more low-cut than her usual t-shirts. This would have looked appropriate in a Perth nightclub, especially combined with her little

shorts. Different shades of blue against blue —
she'd blend in with the water if she fell in.

I think she'd used the twenty minutes to put
on some makeup, too, though it was hard to
tell. Her lips glistened more and appeared
pinker than usual, at least. She smelled good,
too.

I offered her a hand to get into the dinghy,
but she just laughed and leaped in, ignoring it.
"Hop in," she called.

She cruised around to the side of her boat,
where her deckies stood on deck, looking
disgruntled.

"Joe and I are going over for a drink at the
club on Little Rat," she told them. "Keep an
eye on things, please."

The dark-haired one looked grumpy and
didn't say anything.

Frosty Belinda nodded. "We will." She
waved as we headed off, not even cracking a
smile.

"They really don't like me," I told Vanessa,
as soon as we were out of earshot.

She shook her head, her eyes on the water.
"No, it's not that," she said slowly, steering us

around a submerged rock. "They're sick of fishing out here. They want to go home."

The opposite of me. As long as Vanessa's here, I don't want to go anywhere else. I'll be happy to stay on these isolated rocks, as long as I have her.

We beached the dinghy on the northern end of Little Rat, digging the anchor in between the row of other dinghies.

It looked like a party was well under way when we walked into the club together. It turned out that someone's son was getting married, and he'd brought a bunch of mates over from Perth and Geraldton for a buck's party and fishing expedition on the islands. The mates stuck out like bent teeth on a comb. *Like I must have when I first arrived.* Vanessa wasn't the only woman there, but she stood out. Or maybe it was just my eyes that were drawn to her.

One of the Perth guys had brought over a karaoke machine and, after a few drinks, we all proceeded to demonstrate how badly we could sing. Vanessa abstained, laughingly telling me that if she sang we'd all go home.

I went to get Vanessa another drink.

Skipper picked up the microphone as and surprised us all with his rendition of some old KISS song, *I was made for lovin' you*. He sang, he danced and he pulled pouty, kissy faces at everyone until even I wondered whether he was gay or straight, and I knew he had a wife and kids on the mainland. When Skipper's performance was done, we all clapped and cheered, then fell silent for a moment. None of us wanted to be the next one up.

In the momentary lull, the voice of one of the Perth visitors piped up, slurred with beer. "So, you're the stripper. When do we get to see you with your gear off?" The idiot was looking at Vanessa.

We all froze in silence. I was willing to bet that every man in the room had fantasised about her naked, but not a single one of us would have been stupid enough to say it.

Vanessa's knuckles went white around the neck of her empty stubby, her expression as angry as her brunette deckie normally looked. Her eyes were fixed on the table nearest to her and I could almost see the thought process. *In a few seconds, she'll smash the end off that bottle on the edge of the table and gut the idiot like a fish...*

My God, she took out a four-metre tiger shark with a filleting knife. This idiot won't stand a chance. My empty beer bottle slipped from my fingers and smashed on the tiles behind the bar. I couldn't take my eyes off her to pick it up.

Someone pressed a button on the karaoke machine to break the silence. Pink loudly told the room they didn't want to mess with her tonight. *Fuck. What idiot picked a song that was only going to make this worse?*

One of the older skippers laughed. It sounded forced and unnatural. He pounded the idiot so hard on the back he almost knocked him over, not entirely by accident, driving him away from Vanessa. "Ha! Bucks' parties at the Abrolhos don't have strippers. The last stripper we had out here wore huge high heels and wanted to know where the roads and the hotel were..."

A few of the others joined in, helping to tell the story as loudly as possible, to be heard over the music. I knelt down and swept up the broken glass as quickly as I could.

The buck, clearly visible in his newspaper

admiral's hat, was apologising profusely for his mate by the time I reached Vanessa. "I'll get him up as soon as he's sober tomorrow, no matter how hungover, and he'll tell you how sorry he is. Or we'll ship him back to Perth..."

Wordlessly, I handed her a fresh beer and pried the empty bottle from her fingers. I tossed the empty into the bin, out of her reach.

Vanessa tipped the beer up, taking a big drink. She stopped to take a breath, then drank deeply again.

Admiral Buck headed off, distracted by something.

I moved closer to her. "Would you like to head off soon?"

She emptied the beer, wiped her mouth with the back of her hand, and threw the empty into the bin. She opened her mouth to reply and let rip with the mother of all belches.

Well, she drained that beer in less than a minute. No wonder.

A few blokes stared. She covered her mouth with her hand. "Please, excuse me."

She stepped carefully around the table and headed out the door. I started to follow her out, but one of the experienced fishers grabbed my arm.

"Don't," he muttered.

I pulled my arm out of his grasp. "Why the hell not?"

He kept his voice low. "The last bloke who followed her out of the club when she was upset ended up with a broken jaw, before he fell off the cliff and broke a few more bones. Skipper doesn't need to lose another deckie to stupidity."

It took a minute for the details to click in my head. "You mean *Vanessa* pushed Skipper's last deckie off a cliff?"

The old-timer shrugged. "He said he fell. But half an hour before he fell, he told her she should start a whorehouse in her place and she'd earn more on her back than she did fishing. She left here in a hurry, he followed her, and not long after we found him at the bottom of the cliffs. She said she went home to Rat and didn't see him. He says he fell. But if she decked him, he probably deserved it."

I backed away from him, stammering some kind of goodbye, and headed into the darkness outside, switching on my torch. *I'm not stupid enough to insult her. She won't push me off a cliff.*

Instead of following the track to the beach, she'd stumbled through the low scrub to the cliff. She was faster than I would have thought possible and I struggled to catch up to her. When she reached the edge, she stopped, looking out over the dark waves, less than a metre below her feet.

"Hey, the boat's back this way," I called softly. "Or were you thinking of throwing yourself off the cliff?"

I shone my torch at her, so I saw her half turn to give me a look. We both knew that if she jumped off the little cliff, she'd probably just get cold and wet and have to climb back up again.

Unless she landed wrong, like the stupid deckie, or someone pushed her off.

"No." She sniffled. "I want to swim." She sounded fierce.

I got close enough to her to see the tears streaking her cheeks in the torchlight. She swiped at them with her hands.

"You want to swim back to Rat? In the

dark, with the waves and the sharks?" I asked gently.

If she meets up with a shark in her current temper, my money is on her. The shark will be supper for sure. Even a big wave with any sense will only help to carry her home. God help anything that crosses her right now.

"No," she said through gritted teeth. "I want to go home."

I was near enough to touch her. "Shh, it's okay. I'll take you home." I held out my arms to her.

She gave a strangled sob and threw her arms around me, literally crying on my shoulder as I clasped my arms around her back. We just stood there for a while, until she was still and the tears stopped coming.

"C'mon," I whispered. "Let's go find that dinghy."

She held my hand as we walked together down the track to the beach. The dinghy hadn't moved. I stowed the anchor and we both pushed the tinny out into the water. She got in first and I followed. I reached over and started the motor, which purred like mine never did.

She curled up in the bow seat. Her knees were bent on the seat beside her, her feet hanging off the back of the seat. She leaned forward over the bow into the wind, looking like the figurehead on some old ship. I blinked, wondering if I'd had too much beer, to be imagining stuff like this.

"I should drive," she said half-heartedly, making no move to get closer to the motor.

"The dents in my dinghy are from when the engine got flooded by a big wave and I drifted onto a rock," I told her. "Unless you think the same thing's gonna happen tonight, I'm fine to drive."

"They wouldn't dare," she muttered.

Shit, I bet every wave will behave tonight, speeding her home so as not to incur her wrath. Even she thinks so.

I gunned the engine, heading back to Rat.

BELINDA

I sat on deck, watching for dolphins, but Maria soon tired of this and went inside the cabin.

I heard her turn the television on. It sounded like a programme about whales going on land to die. This was not something I wanted to see or hear, so I closed the cabin door quietly and remained outside. I sat on the deck and watched the stars and the water.

The only sounds were the waves sweeping through the anchorage, and the generators on the island. There were no humans outside the buildings. Like us, they planned to wake before the sun had risen, or they were on Little Rat with Vanessa.

I watched a large shark cruise through the anchorage, perhaps looking for sea lions or fish. He turned his head and I saw it was a hammerhead, perhaps the largest I had yet seen. His presence would explain why the dolphins had not come to swim with us yet.

I decided to tell Maria about him, once her whale-death programme was finished.

I stretched out on the deck again. I wanted to be in the water swimming, but even Vanessa's arbitrary orders were to be obeyed. Instead, I watched for rocks burning up in the dark sky high above my head. I had counted six before Maria slammed the cabin door open.

"Sister, the humans know of us. They have heard us sing, they have found bodies of our kind and they are studying them!"

I had never seen her so pale. She would not joke about such a serious matter. I rolled to my feet. *"How do you know this? Have you heard humans discussing us? I have not heard any voices bar yours."*

She gestured frantically with her hand. *"The humans have broadcast a programme detailing the results of their research. Come and see!"*

I followed her doubtfully into the cabin. Maria pointed at the television screen. "*Look. They have even filmed us swimming!*"

I looked, but the figures in the water were not clear. I checked the channel, and found it to be something called Animal Planet, which purported to show programmes on animal behaviour, as opposed to fictional entertainment. I settled down to watch Maria's alarming programme, hoping that whale carcasses would not be shown.

When I saw what the humans considered evidence of mermaids, I couldn't stop laughing. The mermaids they showed had tails like a dugong, webbed fingers and no hair. Also, they were ugly and completely blue. "*Those aren't people of the ocean's gift. Those are humans wearing cosmetics and clothing.*"

Maria was still worried. "*Perhaps the humans had to do this to demonstrate what they thought we looked like, based on their evidence. Still, they know we are here. Look, the body they found was in South Africa!*"

I raised my eyebrows. "*The body the humans claim to have found was a few years ago in South*

Africa. Have you heard of any deaths among our kind in the last ten years? They would have sent Vanessa with Nafula to take care of a lost body. Vanessa has not visited Africa in many years. If the humans have a body they have investigated, it is not one of ours."

The programme ended with humans venturing out in a small vessel to search for mermaids, by using a recording of mermaid voices to call them. I watched this carefully.

"If they had a real recording of our kind, they and their vessel would have been destroyed by our people. This is evidence that the humans know nothing of us. Come, I will show you on Vanessa's machine in the house." I crossed the deck and leaped lightly onto the jetty. I led the way back to Vanessa's blue house. There was no light in the house, so I switched it on. I pressed the button on the little computer machine and the screen glowed in a semblance of life.

A little apprehensive, as I had only seen Vanessa do this and not used the machine myself, I used the device she called a mouse to connect to the internet. I carefully typed out, "mermaid" in the search box that appeared when I clicked the blue letter "e".

I laughed again when I read on the screen a question asking if I had been "fooled" by the Animal Planet "program".

I pointed it out to Maria. *"You see? This is entertainment, as is all you see on that television screen. Here, would you like to know if humans consider mermaids to be real?"*

I carefully typed in, "Are mermaids real" and was rewarded with a statement from a human government department. *"Look. This human agency says that no aquatic humanoids have ever been found."*

Maria looked thoughtfully at the screen. She read more slowly than I did. *"I think that human government department has one of our kind working in it. Our Pacific sisters must have a powerful singer as skilled as Vanessa, who passes for human."*

I considered this. *"Perhaps. Or maybe humans are just not observant, and those who are do not survive long enough to make their observations widely known."*

We both heard the sound of a small motor approaching.

"She is returning. Quick, we must return to the vessel and maintain our watch."

We hurried along the jetty and sat on the

deck. We waved as she went past. She acknowledged us with a nod, but the human she permitted to drive her small boat did not see us.

Maria chose to report on what she had seen. *"We have learned nothing but that humans are gullible and sometimes stupid."*

Out of respect for my sister, I did not voice my thoughts, but I reflected that Maria had more in common with humans than she acknowledged.

JOE

I tied Vanessa's dinghy up at her jetty, then jumped out to offer her my hand. This time, she took it without really noticing, stepping slowly onto the jetty. She kept a hold on my hand as she trudged listlessly back to her house.

As she opened her front door, golden light spilling out onto the decking at her feet, I let go of her and wished her a good night. I started back to my house.

"Please stay," she said quietly.

I turned to look back. She stood in the doorway, haloed in light, but her face was in shadow as she was facing me in the dark.

"I would really appreciate it if you would stay the night with me." Her voice was steady and calm.

I retraced my steps to stand in front of her again. *If I close my eyes, maybe I can deliver the words that I've been rehearsing in my head while we were in the dinghy.* "You're angry and upset and you want me to comfort you. I get that and I'd like to. But you're upset because one fuckwit had the stupidity to say he wanted to see you with your clothes off. A few months ago, I might have been that idiot." I paused for breath and reached out to clasp her hands. "If you'd volunteered to do it, not a single man in that room would have objected, me included. We'd have all held our breath in anticipation until we went blue. I think, if you'd undone the buttons on your shirt and showed them even a glimpse of your bra, every man over 40 in that room would have had a heart attack. We'd have needed the nurse, the rescue helicopter, the Royal Flying Doctor Service and a boatload of defibrillators. And the reason why is because you're beautiful. The first time I saw you in your bathers on deck I thought I'd died and gone to heaven."

I paused for breath and risked a look at her. She smiled faintly, but she didn't say anything.

"You want me to stay and tell you what an amazing woman you are, that I'd be happy with you if I never saw you with your clothes off again. You are an amazing woman, it's hard to believe any human man would have a hope in hell with you. But I'd be lying if I said I didn't want to see you naked again, because seeing you and touching you and fooling around with you is so addictive that you're like a drug. One hit and I'm hooked, the biggest, ugliest groper you ever fished up. And if one day I don't see you, I'll get withdrawal symptoms, as bad as any chemical drug." That's all I managed to say before I choked up and the words wouldn't come out any more.

She cleared her throat. "Please, I'd still like you to stay."

I laughed. "Because you think I'm different to them? I'm not. The only difference is that I want you to take your clothes off in private so I can be selfish and I don't have to share you with anyone else. You don't want me tonight."

I threw my hands up in surrender.

She took a step back into the light, so I could see her face more clearly. Her face was still tearstained, but her impish smile shone through the tears. "For someone who notices so much sometimes, it's amazing how oblivious you can be. You really have no idea." She pulled her shirt up and over her head, letting it dangle from her hand by her side. My head filled with the vision of blue lace that moved with her every breath.

She raised her eyebrows. "How much more do I have to take off to get you to come in and shut the door?" She started to undo the buttons on her shorts.

"What are you doing?" I hissed.

"Baiting a big, stubborn groper, I think," she retorted. She started to slide the shorts down over her hips.

I looked around, but it was too dark to see if anyone else was nearby. "What if someone sees you?"

She looked at me with a puzzled smile. "I'm counting on *you* seeing me, and I'm hoping you'll lock the door behind you, which should take care of everyone else." The shorts slid to the floor and she kicked them aside. I was mesmerised by the sight of the blue lace g-string I'd dreamed about.

She walked slowly toward me, now wearing nothing but blue lace. I couldn't move or take my eyes off her. *This is the girl of my dreams, complete with blue lace underwear.* She clasped her arms around my neck and kissed me, there in the middle of the path.

I didn't know where to put my hands, but I had to get her inside before someone saw her. I grabbed her round the middle, my lips still on hers, and tried to walk us both into the house. She kicked the door shut behind us, pushing my back to it. Pressing up against me, she reached around me to lock the door. I came up for breath, gasping.

She looked into my eyes. "I'm upset because I wanted to kill a man tonight and I didn't. And I would like you to stay because I think your presence may prevent me from killing a man in the morning, when he comes to mumble an apology."

She crossed the kitchen and turned the lock

on the back door, treating me to a clear view of exactly what her g-string didn't cover. *Shit, she does still want me and I've never wanted her so much. How in hell does she look sexier in her underwear than she does naked?*

"Now, we have the house securely to ourselves and all night to enjoy it. What do you suggest we do first?" Her smile was wicked as she reached behind her to undo her bra.

No, not yet! I want to enjoy this for a bit longer. Then I want to help you take it all off…

"Oh, please don't," I begged her.

She looked at me in surprise. "You don't want me to take my clothes off? I thought…" The colour drained from her face.

She thinks I don't want her. Oh God, as if that could ever happen. I struggled with the words. "I've dreamed about this," I began.

Her smile was thoughtful. "You've dreamed about me in my underwear?" She laughed.

Now I was embarrassed. "Yes," I mumbled, not looking at her face.

She moved closer to me, within arm's reach. "Do I ever take it off?" she asked gently.

I felt my face grow hot. *I'm not going to tell*

Vanessa the fantasies I'd constructed in my head about her. "If I'm lucky," I managed to say.

"And what else do we do?" she asked softly.

"We start slow," I began, swallowing hard. My mouth opened, but I couldn't work out what words to say. *How do I explain to this perfect woman that all the fantasies I'd had about her since last weekend involved an incredibly elaborate seduction, until, miracle of miracles, she'd agree to take everything off and sleep with me again? Sex like we'd had last weekend was only ever the climax of my fantasies, right at the end, if I was lucky. If I wasn't lucky, I'd get brought back to reality by a well-aimed rotten lobster or someone banging on my front door, telling me it was time to pull the pots or that their generator had blown. I'd managed to fuck up last weekend and here I am, about to screw up the second chance I never thought I'd get. Why don't you just get one last eyeful of blue lace before you kiss her goodbye?*

My breath caught in my throat as I looked her up and down. My hand was shaking as I ran it lightly across her face and into her hair. Tentatively, I pressed my lips against hers and closed my eyes. I felt her lips part as she took a breath.

I pulled away, cautiously, before opening my eyes. She was right there in front of me. She hadn't moved. Her eyes were laughing at me even before I heard her amused voice. "It might take a while if we go this slow."

For the first time ever, her laughter irritated me. "Haven't you noticed I get tongue-tied around you? You're not making this any easier," I snapped.

Vanessa stopped laughing. Her expression turned gentle. She took my hand and led me to her bedroom, which I'd never seen. Her hands helped me to take my shirt off, then my shorts, so I was standing there in my underwear, just like her.

She was facing me, close enough to touch. Her smile was soft. "Are your dreams different to anything we've done together before?"

I want to give you the best night of your life. I want it to be so good you're still beside me when I wake up in the morning. My voice died and I didn't manage to say a word of it. I nodded, looking down at my feet. *Fuck.*

She took a step closer, so now all I could see was the deep, inviting cleavage between her boobs, edged with blue lace.

"Show me," she whispered. "We have all night. Show me your dreams, and I promise you will be lucky."

I learned that when a man's dreams come true, he yearns for more. At the end of that night with Vanessa, I yearned for sleep, so I could dream about her all over again. With my eyes open.

BELINDA

"What occupies your attention for so long? Surely nothing on land could hold such fascination." Maria's voice came from the cabin.

I responded without taking my eyes from the island. *"Her interaction with the young human fisherman."*

I heard her footsteps on the deck, her voice growing louder as she approached. *"Does their conversation have such great import? I had not thought him a source of significant information. Perhaps her preference for him has been a pretext to pump him for his knowledge. This I would understand."*

I reflected on how best to phrase my response. *"No, it appears that the human is the one engaged in pumping."*

Maria's reaction was immediate. *"What? He knows about us and seeks information about our sisters in the deep?"* Maria came to stand by my side, peering across the water at the window of the blue house.

I tried to caution her before she discerned their interactions. *"Calm yourself. It appears the only information he seeks is whether she derives enjoyment from his attentions. She freely and frequently asserts that she does."*

Maria's anxiety gave way to disgust. *"You have been watching her let him stick a bit of himself inside of her?"*

I tried not to laugh. *"Several bits, actually. Some of his fingers, his tongue, as well as the appendage that is inside her at present. She has expressed considerable pleasure at his repeated penetration of her on at least three occasions. Wait...no, it appears to be four."*

Maria turned away. *"This is disgusting to watch. I do not know how you can stand it. Why does she not close the curtains over the window so that no one witnesses her degradation?"*

"It is too dark for humans to see through the window. Only we can penetrate the darkness to see her

close relations with the human fisherman. Our people do not hide from our sisters in the deep," I called after her.

I heard the splash as Maria went over the side. *"Even this talk of penetration makes me feel unwell, my skin soiled."*

I made my voice reasonable. *"Then do not watch. I will keep watch, in accordance with her orders. Go and wash your imaginary soiled skin in the waves. On your return, please bring me something small for dinner. Small, sweet fish, easily slid down whole. I find I am not unwell at all, but hungry."*

Maria took off into the water, the ripples barely marking her passage.

I turned my eyes back to the bedroom in the blue house. They had changed position again, to one I had not seen before. She was particularly vocal about her enjoyment of this. I wondered idly whether I would also find such a method of joining with a human male equally enjoyable. I dismissed the thought. Necessity would not require me to join with a human male again.

After several hours of energetic activity, they lay exhausted on her bed. Both were naked and lying on their sides, facing the same way. He was so close behind her that a casual arm thrown over her ended in draping his fingers over her breasts. In fact, he was so close behind her that if his present limp appendage were to become engorged with blood again, it would penetrate her without her consent. She wiggled and rubbed her behind against him, so that she was even closer to him than before.

Perhaps she had already given her consent and she was waiting for a firmer response from the human. I reflected on this until I heard a splash from behind me.

Maria returned, replete, carrying a handful of fish as long as her hand. It wasn't until I had eaten my sweet little fish and I was sipping the fiery liquor we had brought from the mainland that a thought occurred to me.

Her coupling with this human was not driven by necessity or duty. What did drive her to lie naked beside him?

I took comfort in the fact that the young human fisherman also did not know the answer to this. Perhaps we were not so different to the humans, after all.

I sipped my fiery drink, feeling it burn as I swallowed. I closed my eyes, reminded of the burn of fires in the past, thinking of flames that, once kindled, could never be extinguished.

Zerafina, my fiery daughter, I will return home to you soon.

JOE

I woke up tangled with Vanessa and the sheets in her bed. What I wanted more than anything was to pick up where we'd left off before, but she was already rolling out of bed, away from me. Someone was knocking hard at the front door and it looked like the sun was up.

I got my shorts on before she was dressed, so I answered the door for her.

Two men stood outside, looking like they had terrible hangovers. One was just recognisable as Admiral Buck minus his newspaper hat. He was also missing an eyebrow and he'd acquired a lot of makeup. The other bloke was the idiot who was lucky to be alive.

"Is Vanessa home? I was told she lived here," Admiral Buck asked loudly, squinting at me.

"She does. I'll go see if she's up." I left them at the door to see if she was dressed yet. She was; wearing a polo shirt buttoned up to the top and pants that came down to just past her knees, she was sitting on the edge of the bed, brushing her hair into a ponytail. She went into the bathroom and washed her face, before following me out to the front door.

She leaned against one side of the doorframe, her arms crossed in front of her chest. "Good morning. What do you want?"

"Matt here wants to apologise for saying bad things about you last night." Buck shoved Matt forward and backed away.

Behind them, I could see Vanessa's formidable deckies watching with interest from the deck of her boat. *If she killed him, they'd take him and dump his body somewhere in the deep, without a qualm. Those two are cold and inhuman, like no one else I've ever met.*

Matt was mumbling his way through a semi-unintelligible apology. The only word I definitely understood was "sorry", which he repeated often.

When he ran down, Vanessa spoke. "You're sorry?" She didn't sound particularly enthusiastic about the idea.

Matt nodded emphatically.

She grabbed him by his shoulders. "Not yet you're not." She brought her knee up between his legs, so hard she actually lifted him off the ground. I winced in sympathy. He made a wordless squeaking noise that sounded like distant dolphins. "Every time you look at an attractive woman and you start getting aroused, you're going to hurt. Then you're going to be sorry. Maybe even sorry enough to make me feel better, because I know you'll never do it again."

She let go of him and he crumpled into a heap on the path.

Her deckies found this hilarious. I could hear their laughter, from the other end of the jetty.

"You," she addressed Buck.

He stayed a safe distance away. "Me?"

"You get your mate here out of my sight before I hurt him worse. He'll want some ice on that." She turned and stalked back into the house, shutting the door firmly behind her. She sagged against the door, her eyes closed.

"Wow. I hope I never offend you," I blurted out. I uncrossed my legs, slowly.

She looked up, opening her eyes. Her smile was rueful as she stood up. "Me too, because I'm not sure I could do that to you. Well, at least it wasn't as messy or as final as using a broken bottle," she said matter-of-factly.

"One of the guys told me something last night..." I began, hesitant but dying to know. "About the deckie Skipper had before me."

"What did they tell you?" Her voice had turned low and cautious.

Oh shit. Shouldn't have said anything. It's too late now.

"They say he fell off a cliff, but that he offended you not long before he fell." I tried to match her cautious tone, but it just came out sounding scared.

"He suggested I was a whore and offered me twenty dollars to sleep with him. When I refused and tried to walk away, he touched me without my permission. I did the same to him as the idiot this morning. Instead of being incapacitated, this only angered him. He tackled me to the ground and he attempted to remove my clothing. My deckhands were nearby and came to my assistance. Maria kicked him in the face, which I believe broke his jaw. Belinda wished to remove some of his appendages and, without being aware of our location, he backed away from her. He fell backwards off the cliff and did himself further damage. He requested our assistance, but I forbade my deckhands from touching him further, either to assist or inflict additional damage. I informed him that if I ever saw him again, I would kill him. Belinda indicated that if she saw him again, she would remove any unnecessary appendages. I'm not sure whether he remembers this, though, as he injured his head in the fall and appeared quite hazy regarding the details before he fell, when he was questioned the following day." She delivered this entire account in a tone devoid of emotion, without looking at me. She took a deep breath and met my eyes. "I don't believe there were any other witnesses, though I am certain that some of the fishermen who were present in the club that night suspect the truth, or some of it."

"The idiot called you a whore and tried to rape you. I'm surprised you didn't want to kill him on the spot, too." *Like the guy last night, who only made an insulting comment. Good thing she didn't have her deckhands with her last night.*

"He attempted to remove my clothing. That is all. I did want to kill him, but I resisted the urge. I left him bleeding in the water, my gift to the sharks." She shrugged. "It's none of my concern that the other fishers chose to assist him."

I imagined the dickhead deckie as like Dean on drugs, desperate for the first decent girl he saw after a long stint in the bush. He'd lived in my shack, done my job…shit, he'd probably watched those old porn films about Debbie. Now I understood why Skipper warned me to keep away from her. Even more amazed, I wondered why she'd picked me.

"You have no idea how happy I am you

decided to sleep with me instead of leaving me to be food for sharks," I said.

She gave a tiny smile. "Well, if you were to call me a whore, I might reconsider feeding you to the sharks. I'm sure the tiger shark we caught on the weekend had some mates who'd like revenge."

I'd been the only one in the water when she went for the shark with a knife. Did she seriously go after it to save me?

"Fuck, I wouldn't want you to be a prostitute. I'd never be able to afford even five minutes with you, if you were. I'd have to rob a bank to get anywhere near you." I looked at her in stunned awe. "And when I think of what we've done together...shit, I must be the luckiest man alive."

Vanessa looked puzzled for a moment before she laughed, sounding relieved. "I can think of something we haven't done yet." She bit her lip. "Would you like to join me in the shower? Unlike the one on the boat, the one in the house is big enough for two."

I followed her out of the kitchen as she started to shed her clothes.

She adjusted the showerhead so that the spray hit the wall. Then she stood with her back to that same wall, her knees apart. "Ready, Joe?"

I stepped into the shower with her. *Oh God, this is a dream I don't want to wake up from.*

When the hot water ran out and the shower turned icy cold, I knew I was awake. But I was still inside her and we weren't stopping for the world. I let the shower freeze my arse off, because it didn't matter. The rest of my body was on fire with love for Vanessa.

BELINDA

"Ensure the vessel is stored and meet me at the airport with the vehicle. We will hide our clothes on board the vehicle and take to the water from a nearby beach. By this time tomorrow, we will be swimming home." Vanessa sounded wistful at the prospect.

"You could still accompany us," Maria suggested. *"You need not fly in a small human aircraft."*

Vanessa smiled. *"I do not like the aircraft, but I would like one more day on land at these islands before I return home. I will risk a flight for the additional time, to ensure the house here is properly packed up to remain unoccupied until it is next required."*

I said the words as I thought them. *"And also to spend time with the young human fisherman."*

Vanessa's voice held a warning. "*I enjoy the human's company and we still owe him for the favours he has done for us. The least I can offer is a proper farewell.*"

I tried to explain. "*You have permitted the human to use your body without restraint. Surely this is payment enough for any services he has rendered to us?*"

Vanessa's laughter rang out across the anchorage. "*Belinda, I make far freer use of his body than he does of mine. It is more likely that I owe him a personal favour for the joy he gives to me. I wish you a good voyage and I will see you at the airport tomorrow.*"

She stepped from the vessel to the jetty and assisted us in casting off the ropes. She waved as we moved the *Siren* into the anchorage channel.

"And he does have a damn fine arse!" she called across the water. The sound of her laughter followed us as she proceeded back down the jetty to her house.

Despite myself, I smiled. She was an elder among our people, but today she sounded as silly as the sixteen-year-old child who dared to defy the entire Elder Council.

JOE

"Good morning, Sleeping Beauty." I heard Vanessa's voice and felt her lips start to kiss mine. I wasn't sure if I was awake or dreaming, but I knew I wanted her.

I felt her slide down onto me, hotter and wetter than ever before. *Oh God, this dream's good.* It had to be a dream, because it felt like I wasn't wearing a condom...*Oh shit.*

I opened my eyes, to see her rapturous face over her bouncing boobs.

"Vanessa, wait, wait," I begged her. "We have to stop." I tried to lift her off me.

She let me succeed a little way, before sliding right back down onto me, pushing her weight down on me so I drove deeper inside her. *God, she feels good.*

"Don't ask me to stop now. Neither of us has come yet, and it feels so good," she murmured.

If she wouldn't get off of me, I had to check. I hesitated, then tried to slide my hand underneath her, pushing my fingers up inside her, too. She moaned, rocking her hips against me. I felt around desperately for the condom that wasn't there. *Skin on skin on skin, hot and wet and hard...*

I felt her shuddering orgasm, as she squeezed me hard inside her and moved her hips faster. I pulled my fingers out of her – quite an effort. *So hot and tight and wet...oh my God...*I felt like I'd exploded inside her, it was that incredible. I groaned when she lifted her hips to slide up off me. She quickly moved down and started licking me clean.

"Oh God, Vanessa, we had sex without a condom. What if you get pregnant?" I gasped.

*Lick, lick, lick...*She took a deep breath, put my whole dick in her mouth and sucked on me while she pulled me out slowly, leaving me limp. She licked her lips and smiled.

"Please, I didn't want you to have any regrets," I begged.

"I won't get pregnant for sleeping with you this morning. I can't," she said.

"But it only takes the once to put you at risk..." I started to say.

She slid up my body, skin to skin, until we were face to face. "If we spent the rest of the day having sex, without using a single condom, I couldn't conceive a child. No matter how many times you came inside me, you can't get me pregnant." Her eyes bored into mine, as if they were trying to convey a message even if her words didn't get through to me.

After a moment, she moved off me and stood up, walking in the direction of the bathroom. As I watched her go, my head spinning from the most heavenly awakening ever, I found myself wishing she was wrong.

If I could pick the perfect woman to carry my child, Vanessa, I'd want it to be you.

Now I knew I had to be dreaming.

Yeah, what woman would want the father of her child to be a sparky who still lives with his folks and has no assets to speak of? You're still dreaming, mate.

BELINDA

Maria and I watched the vessel being secured for storage until the next fishing season. Both of us fervently hoped that we would not be required to crew the *Siren* for another season. We wished to remain with our families, she with her partner and I with my daughter.

We shared our last human-cooked meal, chilli mussels in the restaurant with the curious human. He was not working this time, his duties undertaken by a human woman instead. She permitted us to eat in peace.

We drove to the car park at the airport and shared a beer as we waited for the small plane to arrive. We finished the beer and I wished I had thought to bring a bottle of whiskey, for one last fiery burn before all was cool water once more.

The sun was sinking in the sky when Vanessa's plane landed. She walked slowly to the car, opened the rear door and sat behind me.

I made a polite enquiry. *"Did you farewell the human properly?"*

She replied in the affirmative, her smile dreamy.

I noticed a patch of white on her otherwise immaculate shirt. *"You have some white fluid on your clothing,"* I told her.

She looked at her clothing and shrugged. *"Soon we will not need human clothing. Within the hour, we will be swimming home. Our people are calling."*

JOE

"Looks like the plane's early," Vanessa said, annoyed, as the sound of the aircraft engine came closer. "Oh well, I guess I'm ready." She picked up one bag and I grabbed the other before she could reach for it. She smiled at me. "Let's head out to the airstrip, then."

It was a long walk down the coral shingle track, but today of all days, when I wanted to draw it out, it seemed to take no time at all.

The six-seater plane was down by the time we reached it, already loading up. Some of the passengers were seated inside, looking at us through the windows. They didn't look like anyone I'd met – maybe they were fishers from

North Island or the Wallabis.

"You're early," Vanessa called to the pilot. "I didn't think you were going to be here before four."

"Oh, this isn't your flight," the pilot replied. "This is a tourist flight, but we're just picking up some gear the Fisheries guys needed to take urgently back to the mainland." He lifted up a foam esky and loaded it onto the plane. "Your plane is due to take off in about ten minutes. We'll probably cross in the air."

"Oh," she huffed, dropping her bag on the gravel. Her shoulders slumped.

It was roughly a half-hour flight out here and it took at least fifteen minutes to walk the track back to camp. "Let's go wait in the departure lounge," I suggested.

Vanessa looked where I was pointing. "You mean the shelter shed? Sure, let's go sit down and wait."

We crossed the airstrip and crunched back to the shed. Three walls and a roof in cream-painted steel, with a couple of aluminium benches. I'd heard from some of the old-timers that it was luxury compared to the old rusted rainwater tank that used to be here, but it was still pretty basic.

I lifted her bags onto one aluminium bench and sat beside her on the other.

"It's funny, but I never thought I'd be sad to leave this place," she said quietly.

It was my turn to laugh. "You'll miss the rocks, the wind, the wailing birds and the endless sound of the waves?"

"Yeah, some of that. Probably not the sound of the waves, though." She shook herself. "It probably doesn't help that I don't like flying."

I look at her, incredulous. "You don't like flying? Why didn't you go back in the *Siren* yesterday with your crew, then?"

"I get seasick, remember." She took a breath and let it out slowly. "And I wanted one more night here."

I struggled not to think about what we'd done in that one more night. Instead, I tried to summon the courage to ask her the one thing I hadn't been able to figure out. We both watched the tourist plane take off to the south, before I opened my mouth.

"Why did you pick me? Of all the people out here, out of everyone you know, why did you choose to spend so much time with me?" I stumbled over the words. Even now, there were some I just couldn't say.

She looked at me and smiled. "You have a good sense of humour. You're brave when someone needs your assistance, even if it puts your own safety at risk." I was willing to bet she was remembering the night with the hammer. "You enjoy life and you're seldom sad for long. You are sweet, honest, polite, kind and helpful. You are a genius with all things electrical, and with my dodgy house, it's always a good idea to have tradesmen nearby. You are thoughtful, careful to think before you do something, so you won't hurt someone." Her smile turned mischievous. "And you have a damn fine arse, which I noticed the first time I saw you."

I knew the right answer to this was to go into paeans of praise about her, but I could do that till her plane arrived and I'd still have more to say. And she still hadn't really answered my question. I tried again.

"But why did you choose to...sleep with me?" I stammered out.

She bit her lip. "Well, after we'd had such vigorous sex, I was too exhausted to sleep anywhere else, and it was convenient to have you nearby when I woke up so we could do it again..." Her smile was wicked now.

I opened my mouth to try to articulate what I really wanted to know. It was hard to find the words and I knew I only had a short time left to do it. The pressure didn't make it any easier.

I realised she'd been teasing me when she continued, a little more seriously. "I think it was the way you adored me with your eyes, with such passion and intensity, but you were too polite to say anything about it."

She's forgotten about the time I told her I wanted to bend her over a bench and fuck her from behind...

Her cheeks reddened. "I was curious to find out what that passion and intensity would feel like if you used the rest of your body." She closed her eyes and bit her lip again.

I jumped to my feet, disappointed and angry and not entirely sure why. "You slept with me to satisfy your curiosity?" It sounded so clinical, so cold, when the reality had been anything but.

She stood up, too, and met my eyes. "The first time, yes. After that, I was more interested in satisfying a number of other desires." She smiled ruefully. "Including the desire to see your fine arse in the flesh and get my hands on it..."

She pressed up against me and kissed me, pushing me up against the shed wall. I kissed her back and held her close. There was nothing cold about this. I seriously considered laying her down on one of the benches, so we could do it one last time...in broad daylight, in public, with a plane coming at any moment...and I realised I didn't care, I wanted her that much.

It was like she could read my mind when she pulled away from me, sinking down so I thought she was moving toward the bench. I froze in panic.

"That looks uncomfortable. Let me help you with that," she murmured. I realised she was on her knees in front of me, unzipping my jeans so I stuck out in a poor imitation of the windsock behind her. Her hands were on the back of my jeans...and then I was inside her mouth. I didn't care what I looked like anymore, it felt so good.

My knees went weak and I tangled my fingers in her hair, unable to think as she sucked the whole length of me in and out of her mouth. She didn't stop until she'd sucked me dry. My head was spinning as she zipped my jeans up again, before she stood up, wiping a hand across her mouth. The buzzing in my head resolved into the loud engine of a plane, as it sped by, landing on the runway.

Vanessa had a bag in each hand, now. She kissed my cheek and pulled away. "Goodbye," she called as she ran out of the shed, across the airstrip to her plane. I was too stunned to move while she was still within reach, and by the time I reached my arms out to hold her one last time, she was under the wing of the plane, loading up her bags.

She turned and waved, blowing me a kiss as she climbed into the seat beside the pilot of the two-seater plane, hidden from my sight. The pilot checked her plane, then got in and started back down the runway, taking Vanessa away from me.

SIRENA

"Welcome home, Sirena."

I breathed deep at the sound of my name again, cool water flooding my gills. *"Thank you Maria, Apalala. It's wonderful to be back. Girls, within the year you will have a new sister. Once we have reported to the other elders, we must go to the Nursery Grounds and prepare for her arrival."*

"And what of the fisherman, the human we saved?" Apalala asked the question as only a healer would.

I was complacent. *"He will not remember, for he does not know."*

We swam in silence between the mainland and the islands.

When we reached the islands, I slowed for a moment, permitting my daughters to continue without me. I assured them I would not linger long.

I surfaced to look at the island, to see once more the man and the home it was time to leave behind. For a moment, I felt the ghost of heat between my legs at the memory. But I no longer had legs, my flesh shaped once again into a tail.

I found the word in the language that would soon fade from my tongue again, along with my human habits, thoughts and name. "Goodbye."

I turned my tail, arced high over the water and dove deep.

JOE

In the dark, I sat on the cliffs, looking out toward the reefs I could only hear as the breakers crashed unceasingly. *Will she be back next season? Will I come back next season?*

I looked down at my phone again. Skipper had sent me a message from Geraldton, asking me to come back next year as his deckie, not anyone else's. Apparently some of the other fishers had been talking about hiring me. Because I was lucky. Of course I'd agree, just for the chance to see Vanessa again.

I heard a splash nearby and saw a flash of reflected moonlight on wet skin, a tail breaking the water before going under. It looked too big to be a sea lion. Again, I heard the sound like dolphins. I couldn't see, but pressed the button for my phone camera, pointing it at the noise. I could look at it on a computer later, to see if I could lighten the picture up enough to make out what the dolphins were doing.

Goodbye.

I heard the word in her voice, as if it were drifting in the wind and not just an echo in my own head.

Another splash and the dolphin sounds finished. I switched the camera off and trudged back to camp for a beer.

I sat down at my wonky kitchen table. I had a beer and chased it with another. *I'm going to look her up as soon as I get to Perth. I'll look in the phone book, Google her…Oh fuck. I don't even know her last name. What if I never see her again?* A big black pit opened up under my ribs.

I stumbled to the fridge for another beer. *How many beers does it take to fill a gaping black hole of despair?*

By dawn, I'd finished all the beer in the fridge and my head wasn't getting any brighter. I put a case of warm beer from the veranda in the fridge and passed out while I was waiting for it to chill.

Skipper woke me up to help him pull the pots in a dim haze. I moved like a zombie on autopilot, winching them up, unloading the catch, baiting the pots and setting them again. When we were done, I stumbled back to my shack and found I had a fridge full of cold beer. I cracked one open.

I sat on my veranda with a six-pack, looking out over the anchorage, like the night I'd first met Vanessa, and drank. When the beer was gone, I went back in for more. I sat in the kitchen, not wanting to look at the empty jetty where the *Siren* wasn't. I looked out the back window instead.

I saw her generator shed, where she'd threatened me with a rusty hammer. I reached for another beer and didn't stop drinking until it was too dark to see the shed. At some point, I passed out again. In a soggy dream, Skipper dragged me out of my shack to go pull the pots. Maybe it really happened, I don't know. This time we kept them on deck, not baiting them up again. He said something about meeting his quota, time to go home.

When I got home to my shack, I loaded up every last beer from the veranda into the fridge. Then I started drinking again.

Some time after dark, I woke up with a warm beer still half full in my hand. I could smell fish.

"Oi," said Skipper.

I mumbled some sort of reply. I meant to say *Fuck off and leave me alone,* but even in my beer haze I remembered this bloke was my boss.

"Brought you some dinner. You haven't eaten in days. We're done – we'll pack up and head out, day after tomorrow. I've booked your flights back to Perth. You can go back and sober up. I'll see you again next season."

A plate of fish was put in front of me on the table. I looked at it blearily. *Was there one plate or two? Or was it three?*

"Baldchin groper, tastiest fish in the sea," Skipper said. "Enjoy, mate."

That's what Vanessa said.

I grabbed for the warm beer and took a big mouthful. It had to be the worst beer I'd ever tasted. I turned the can to look at the label. *Fuck, that's the Swan Gold that looked like it was older than me. It tastes like cat's piss.*

I made it to the kitchen sink before I threw up.

I opened the fridge, wiping my mouth, looking for something to chase the taste away. The fridge was empty.

I staggered out to the veranda, looking for more beer, but I only found empty boxes. *Fuck, I drank it all.*

The next two days I had the hangover from hell and vomited it all back up again. The last thing on my mind was dolphins as I hawked my guts up. I even managed not to think of Vanessa.

Skipper threatened to take me to the plane in the wheelbarrow if I didn't walk, so I staggered out to the airstrip myself on the last day, one bag in each hand.

I threw up one last time in the airsick bag on the plane, just after we took off. The pilot didn't say anything.

When I got home to Perth, I slept. I didn't want to do anything else.

SIRENA

"To the west, what have you found?" Elder Darma asked formally.

"They have little or no information about changes and they are undertaking no research to obtain more. The changes have had little effect on them as yet. I do not recommend further information gathering will yield anything in the west," Elder Nafula responded.

Attention turned to Elder Indah.

"To the north?"

Elder Indah hesitated, but her response was sad. *"The changes are greatest in the north, but are not regarded with much concern above the surface. The humans are focused on politics and immigration on the water's surface, not the changes deep below it. I fear the northern humans will not devote their attention to their world beneath the waves until it is too late."*

Elder Darma turned her eyes on me before she spoke. *"And to the east?"*

I lifted my head to voice our best hope. *"The Australian humans are also concerned about the politics in the north, but the changes to their coastal waters have come to their attention. They have observed the warming temperatures, the changes to fish numbers and storm patterns, but they do not presently look for the underlying causes of their observed changes. They appear to be willing to look at this in detail, however, but it will take some time before this occurs, or the factors are associated. I think the east offers the most promise for information in the future…"*

"So we are to conclude that the humans are woefully unaware of the changes taking place in the world around them?" Elder Cantrella interrupted. *"Changes which may mean the end of their survival?"*

"So it seems, yes," I replied mildly. *"It does not necessarily follow that the end of their survival will mean the end of ours. The ocean's gift will ensure our survival, even if the oceans reclaim the land from the humans."*

"We cannot long outlive them. We are dependent on

them for our children, and their demise will result in ours. We still require them to conceive our young. Without offspring, we will not survive." Elder Sunitha sounded frightened.

Elder Darma's voice delivered my conclusions. "*So we are left with one course of action. We must maintain contact with the humans, observe their research and attempt to guide it, so that at least some of them may survive and so shall we. We must also make contact with other communities in other oceans, to see if other sisters of the ocean's gift are better informed than we. And we must plan for contingencies, to preserve human technologies even if the humans themselves are lost, so that our people may still survive. Elder Sirena, whom do you suggest we assign to these tasks?*"

I drew a cool, salty breath and said, "For *technology, I would assign such a task to Maria. She has greater knowledge and experience with human technologies than most. She has lived successfully among them, too. For contact with other oceans, I recommend caution, for their societies are very different to ours. I trust you will send diplomatic elders for such a delicate task. Liaison with humans will be my responsibility, once more.*"

"This task is urgent. How can you undertake it, carrying a child? You cannot leave her until she is weaned, and then you cannot leave her without a teacher. You must remain with the child, and choose another to go in your place." Elder Darma sounded worried.

I attempted to reassure her. *"The humans will not make great advances for some years yet. I will go once the child is weaned."*

Elder Cantrella spoke up, as I knew she would. *"Our people must be hidden at all costs. You may need to live on land among humans for a considerable time."*

I hid my smile. *"I have managed on several occasions to live among them. Even the human man who conceived this child does not know of her or of us. I will do whatever is necessary to protect my people."*

Elder Darma was disappointed, but she knew it was fruitless to oppose me. *"Then needs must. You will proceed as outlined. Remember the survival of our people rests with you, and possibly the survival of the humans, too."*

I imbued my words with power. *"I will not forget."*

JOE

I woke up, knowing it was time to leave for another remote site again. I barely had time to pack my field gear before I had to board the next plane up north. This time it was different. I couldn't forget the Abrolhos, because every time I put on my steel-capped boots, they stank of dead lobster.

Dean met me in the airport, waiting for our charter flight. "How was fishing?" he asked.

"The fishing was good," I told him, my voice flat.

"Did you get to swim with the dolphins? Skipper said there were heaps out there this year." He sounded wistful, like he wished he'd been Skipper's deckie instead of me.

"No, but I got a video of them playing around at night." I pulled out my phone and found the video I'd recorded and not looked at since. I handed it over to him.

"Mate, it's all black," he told me, handing the phone back. It took me a minute to realise he was talking about the video on my phone.

"Hang on a sec." I played with the editing software for a bit, lightening up the picture until I could see the difference between the waves, the water surface and the beach. "Try it again."

He hit play and watched it, his mouth open. I could hear the dolphin sounds. When it finished, he played it over.

"What were the dolphins doing?" I asked.

"Those aren't dolphins, just the sound of dolphins in the background." He laughed. "You had me for a second there, mate. It looks like the end of a bad porn film. I'd like to borrow the porn flick you taped it off, though. She looks hot."

I played the video and watched it. My jaw dropped, too.

I watched Vanessa rise from the water, moonlight glistening on her bare skin, and whisper her goodbye. Then she curved across the waves as gracefully as any dolphin, her tail unmistakeable as it splashed down behind her, fracturing the moonlight on the water to the depths of my dark thoughts. Further out, I saw two similar-sized tails clear the water and vanish.

Oh shit!

THE TALE CONTINUES IN THE NEXT BOOK IN THE SERIES, *OCEAN'S INFILTRATOR*

ABOUT THE AUTHOR

Demelza Carlton has always loved the ocean, but on her first snorkelling trip she found she was afraid of fish.

She has since swum with sea lions, sharks and sea cucumbers and stood on spray drenched cliffs over a seething sea as a seven-metre cyclonic swell surged in, shattering a shipwreck below.

Demelza now lives in Perth, Western Australia, the shark attack capital of the world.

The *Ocean's Gift* series was her first foray into fiction, followed her suspense thriller *Nightmares* trilogy. She swears the *Mel Goes to Hell* series ambushed her on a crowded train and wouldn't leave her alone.

Want to know more? You can follow Demelza on Facebook, Twitter, YouTube or her blog, Demelza Carlton's Place at:

www.demelzacarlton.com

Books by Demelza Carlton

Siren of Secrets series

Ocean's Secret (#1)
Ocean's Gift (#2)
Ocean's Infiltrator (#3)

Siren of War series

Ocean's Justice (#1)
Ocean's Widow (#2)
Ocean's Bride (#3)
Ocean's Rise (#4)
Ocean's War (#5)
How To Catch Crabs

Nightmares Trilogy

Nightmares of Caitlin Lockyer (#1)
Necessary Evil of Nathan Miller (#2)
Afterlife of Alana Miller (#3)

Mel Goes to Hell series

The Devil's Work (#1)
See You in Hell (#2)
Mel Goes to Hell (#3)
To Hell and Back (#4)
The Holiday From Hell (#5)
All Hell Breaks Loose (#6)
The Devil Goes to Heaven (#7)

Romance Island Resort series

Maid for the Rock Star (#1)
The Rock Star's Email Order Bride (#2)
The Rock Star's Virginity (#3)
The Rock Star and the Billionaire (#4)
The Rock Star Wants A Wife (#5)
The Rock Star's Wedding (#6)
Maid for the South Pole (#7)
Jailbird Bride (#8)

Romance a Medieval Fairytale series

Enchant: Beauty and the Beast Retold
Dance: Cinderella Retold
Fly: Goose Girl Retold
Revel: Twelve Dancing Princesses Retold
Silence: Little Mermaid Retold
Awaken: Sleeping Beauty Retold
Embellish: Brave Little Tailor Retold
Appease: Princess and the Pea Retold
Blow: Three Little Pigs Retold
Return: Hansel and Gretel Retold
Wish: Aladdin Retold
Melt: Snow Queen Retold
Spin: Rumpelstiltskin Retold
Kiss: Frog Prince Retold
Reflect: Snow White Retold
Roar: Goldilocks Retold
Cobble: Elves and the Shoemaker Retold